The Day of the Funeral

Nicole Paton Schofield

DEDICATION

For Stuart, James & Caitlyn.

CONTENTS

ACKNOWLEDGMENTS

I would like to thank the people that spent endless time editing, proofreading, designing and publishing this book for me. As well as my family for their patience when I was absent in pursuit of my dream and I hope this encourages them to follow theirs.

1 WAKING UP

I can feel the sun warming me through the open vertical blinds. My skin feels like it's burning as I lay here willing it to stop, I just want to go back to sleep. Covering my arm with the blanket I try to protect it but it's too late, my arm now feels scorched. I can't hear the usual clattering sound coming from the cheap plastic strips that would announce that the window is open. "That must mean the A/C is on, going to be a hot one today," I think to myself

Relief floods me at the thought of not having to listen to kids with their car stereo bass cranked up to ridiculous pulse pounding volumes, cruising down the six lane road that runs in front of our house, but it is so bright in the room that another annoyance is keeping me from reclaiming my sleep. "Damn you" I think, cursing those stupid blinds, "damn you for not doing your job!", "Sun's getting in" I somewhat slur out loud.

As I roll over a bigger nuisance is awaiting me in the shape of a big black 70 pound, eleven year old ball of love, whose sole purpose right now is to get me out of bed so he can shit on a neighbor's lawn. Oh and let's not forget I have the joy of picking up his steaming mess, usually while someone looks on with a defiant arms folded stare as if to say, "That's right, you better pick up after your dog." As if I would ever not do my law(n) abiding duty.

We have many dogs in our townhouse community, which is ironic considering that there is a clause in our lease stating no pets allowed; and not everyone is as diligent about this directive. In the eleven years I have owned my mutt I think there has been one or two occasions that I haven't pooped and scooped and of those times it was because I had either lost my bag on the walk due to wind or not paying attention, or I had thrown his parcel away in a public garbage can thinking he was done, but in these cases I always go home get a bag and return to the scene of the crime.

My eyes are not yet open but I can feel his on me. And here comes the nose. As if on cue the Lab is digging under the covers on my side of the bed searching for my limp hand. Usually if I don't move or open my eyes he will nudge me with his wet nose and lie on the floor for a little while until I get up, leaving me alone so that I can have a few more minutes. The fact that he is more determined than usual makes me believe that it must be after 7AM.

He has started licking my hand, his big pink tongue is warm and wet and I am disgusted. Hey, I love my dog like a family member but my other family members don't soak me with their saliva. "Buster!" I snap, now a little more awake, "GO!" and point firmly to the bedroom door meaning for him to leave me alone.

I wipe my now drenched hand on the beige fleur de lis patterned fitted sheet of my mattress and pull the covers over my head. The blanket has become threadbare and the foam that fills it has pushed beyond the material border that has kept it inside for almost 20 years. It scratches my face and doesn't do much good to keep the sun out as it is almost transparent, allowing the sun to shine through it.

I feel something tugging at my subconscious. Is today Saturday? I can't figure out what day it is. Was I at work yesterday? I can't remember, that's unusual my mind is completely blank. I risk a peak and look at the clock, it's 8:58AM and Tuesday, according to my clock radio. "Oh shit!" I gasp, what the hell am I thinking, I still have to walk the dog, get the lunches ready, and why isn't anyone up?

I jump out of bed and start to grab some clothes from the footboard of our faux wood sleigh bed, when I see it. His side is untouched. His two pillows still neatly fluffed and sitting against the headboard, the blanket still covering his side of the mattress, I am a very still sleeper and rarely disturb his side if he is not there.

Starring at the bed I realize Steve didn't sleep in the bed last night. He hasn't done that in a while. Standing there confused, that feeling has returned, that pulling at my brain and clenching in the pit of my stomach like I have forgotten something huge. What is going on? I am bewildered and starting to get frustrated. What have I forgotten? Then the dreadful pang hits me. Steve is dead, my husband didn't sleep in our bed last night because he died three days ago, and today is his funeral.

I am standing here at the foot of our bed and without thinking about it I have picked up his shirt that was hanging off the footboard. Wringing the shirt that is in my hands I am not sure quite what to do, a panic rising in the back of my throat. Looking down I see it is the shirt I had laid out and ironed for him to be ... what? Laid to rest? Not buried, he wants, no wanted, to be cremated and the ludicrousness of ironing his shirt is suddenly very amusing. In a few hours this very shirt will be a part of a pile of Steve ashes and I spent 45 minutes making sure it was wrinkle free.

I start to giggle an almost maniacal sound escaping me. In our 16 years of marriage I have never ironed unless I had to. Usually saying, "Throw it in the dryer for five minutes then it will be good." I hate to iron, not sure if it is the standing or the leaning over the board, I just detest it and find it to be a tedious task. Maybe it is because in all those 50's movies or shows the woman always seemed to be ironing, an image I deplore, or it might be I just don't have the patience when I could be doing something I feel is more useful with my time, but for some reason last night I persuaded myself I had to send him off in a stiff shirt.

Honestly, the whole thing didn't seem right. I'm sure he would have preferred a cotton T-shirt and some jeans, but his mother had insisted scoffing, "You have to be respectful, don't you have a suit for 'im" in her Manchester accent. Nobody is even going to see him for God's sake, the casket is to be closed.

God how I can't wait for all of this to be over, I hate wishing time away these days it seems so precious to me, but I want everyone to just leave me alone to get on with it, get on with what? Being alone I guess.

I think of my grandmother telling me a story shortly after my grandfather had passed away. The story was of a man that was walking up to her house, she had spotted him about 100 yards down the street, he was wearing a Six Flags coat and hat, which probably doesn't seem weird but she lives in Scotland, they don't have Six Flags there. She was convinced that she was looking at her dead spouse! After all, who on the whole island would have that get up?

It turned out it was my uncle's dad. You see, my uncle worked at Six Flags and gave hats and jackets to his dad and his father in law, my grandfather. Seeing what she thought was my dead grandfather scared her half to death, but grandma McGhee was a tough old broad, she shook it off and went on without him, just like I would have to now.

"How will I do it Steve?" I ask myself and in reply I hear his voice in my head saying; "You only get one." A smile spreads across my face and at the same time tears are threatening to spill down my cheeks. He used to say that whenever there was something expensive to replace involved. This time, however, there was no replacement.

I can recall the Christmas we bought our son Jordan an iPhone. It was all the kid wanted, all he had talked about for the whole month of December, but money was tight and he was convinced that he wouldn't get one. It was hard to watch him as his friends got whatever they wanted and Jordan was looked at as the "poor kid". He opened that iPhone on Christmas morning and his eyes lit up. Even before he had opened the box his dad had piped up with his deep voice, "You only get one kiddo, so look after it okay?" Jordan nodded enthusiastically as he cradled the new gadget.

It was only a few days later I caught him throwing the phone at the floor making it bounce in its new rubber case. "WHAT ARE YOU DOING?!" I yelled horrified. He turned to me innocently and said, "Mom, relax, it's protected." I could have wrung his 13 year old neck. "No, it's not! You think that piddly little twenty dollar case is going to save your phone from you deliberately throwing it at the ground?" I look closer at the phone and the case is just a black rubber cover with a random diagonal design cut into the rubber, it is not made of Kevlar or some kind of indestructible material. Not waiting for his answer I went on, "There is a difference between dropping it and you whipping it at the floor intentionally. So stop doing that" was my response instead. He stopped.

He did look after that phone for a couple of years and in the end it was a trip to a friend's cottage that finally proved too much for the little phone that could. It fell out of his pocket and into the river as he was getting into a kayak. After using an oar and burying it deeper under the river bed from several failed retrieval attempts, the damn thing still turned on, but the screen was damaged. Apple should adopt Timex's old slogan; "It takes a licking and keeps on ticking".

Once home from the cottage his dad went out to the store and came back with another iPhone, same model, not the latest phone, but I'll be damned he broke his own rule and that time Jordan only got two!

I close my eyes and raise the now twisted shirt to my face. Breathing in, I can smell him as though he were in the room with me, a mixture of Drakkar Noir and Axe deodorant. Drakkar Noir I once heard someone refer to as a poor man's cologne, well, we were not at all wealthy. That was his winter smell, if I had held a summer T-shirt it would be Azzarro assaulting my nasal cavity.

I never had the heart to tell him that I detested the sickly sweet scent. His Nin had bought him that in his teenage years and I could never take away the attachment he had to it because of her. Dear Nin, that was his name for his maternal grandmother. When she was alive she was like his best friend. Steve could do no wrong in her eyes and vice versa. She was the only person I had ever truly been jealous of. That may sound ridiculous, but they had a love for each other that I had never seen. It wasn't "pervy" or anything, just beautiful and pure but above all unconditional, truly unconditional love.

Whenever she would go home to England it was heartbreaking, he would fall apart knowing that one of the times he said goodbye to her it would be the last. I think she was the only person in his too short life I never saw Steve get mad at, and at some point or other, he was mad at everybody. It hurt sometimes to think that she could do no wrong, but me, well I was just a "psycho bitch" at times he had no problem hurtling insults at. He had mostly been an angry man with a short fuse.

Lowering the dress shirt I realize all of my hard work ironing the night before has now been undone. The shirt was now a wrinkled white mass, and the kid from the funeral home was coming around this afternoon, "To hell with it!" I think, and decide at that moment that my earlier idea of a T-shirt and jeans is the way to go. I would deal with my mother in law later on the subject of proper "send off" attire.

She had already started in when I said no visitation. That is what Steve wanted. He had explicitly told me while still alive, during the time that we were writing our wills, that if I or the kids wanted to gawk at his dead body, then go ahead, but no one else, and definitely not a procession line of people he hadn't seen in years. In short; if you couldn't bother with him in life, he didn't want to bother with you in death. I am not sure if he was unsympathetic to the act of making amends or if he didn't care.

As I make my way across the room to his third drawer, still on my T-shirt mission, my big toe catches on something sending a wave of pain through my foot that feels like it was threatening to rip the nail right off. I crumple to the floor scared to look at the toe, with my eyes closed I cradle my foot with both hands and rock back and forth all the while doing my labor breathing, you know what I mean, the "whew whew, oh my God I think I am going to die the pain is so bad". Convinced my toe is now hanging by a thread I force myself to look at it. The nail is lifted slightly and a thin line of blood can be seen forming, but I think I will get to keep the toe. Well, thank you Dr. Andrews; such a drama queen!

So what the hell had been able to bring a grown woman to her knees? A stupid book on Java programming that was about a thousand pages thick! I had been asking Steve for months to clean up his side of the bed. When we moved his computer desk from his side of the room, where he had been able to look out the window, to the wall at the foot of the bed, there was a lot of old junk left over that I didn't know what to do with. He didn't want it to be a part of his new setup so, there it stayed.

There were quite a few computer programming books, old files and piles of useless papers with information that meant nothing to me on them contained in this heap. Steve had said, "Leave it in a pile and I will sort through it later." He was the one that went through life not worrying about making a mess because he would "deal with it later". That was his answer for cleaning up, "Deal with it later", or maybe that was code for "She will clean it up". "Well it's later." I mutter to myself sitting on the floor cradling my throbbing toe and pouting. "It's later now Steve!" I say a little louder to the empty room.

I can feel my blood pressure rising and the anger building inside of me, my hands now on my knees my nails digging into my own flesh. My face burns and a white hot rage comes over me that I have never felt before. I feel abandoned like he has done this to me on purpose, and lost, not sure what to do next but above all I feel guilty and I don't know why. How dare he, how could he leave me on my own like this? What was I supposed to do now without him? "IT'S LATER NOW YOU ASSHOLE!" I yell and pick up that fat stupid book that almost severed my toe and throw it, it flies through the air and the spine dents the drywall across the room.

Getting to my feet I pick up as many papers as I can with his stupid handwriting on them, I don't know what these are and don't care. I tear them in half and throw them at the bed we had shared. They don't go very far fluttering in the air then silently landing on the comforter, which is disappointing, but I'm not done, I want to do some real damage, if anything those pathetic papers have made me even angrier. I send the stapler sailing across the room smashing against the wall showering little metal slivers down on Buster, who has returned to see what all the commotion is about.

After surveying the scene he decides it is safer in the hall and he backs out of the room with his ears down and tail between his legs. "Good idea dog." I pick up what had been Steve's survival bag from his pile of junk, it is full of all of his gear for hunting that he would never get to use. I rip the bag open whipping it back and forth sending the contents all over the room, once it has emptied to the point I can throw it I heave the bag into the air knocking over a lamp that sits on his side table.

Collapsing onto his side of the bed, I dissolve into tears. I ache so much. I want him so bad. Just one more touch. Just one more embrace. I cry until I can't anymore, every time I breath in I can smell him on his pillow, that damn mixture of Drakkar Noir and Axe, it hurts so much that no words could even begin to explain the emptiness and the overwhelming feeling that I will never be whole again. Because I won't, half of me is gone forever. He took a powder, went to the great concert in the sky, passed away, passed on, he is dead.

After what seems like hours of fetal position sobbing I look around at the wreckage that had moments earlier been my somewhat tidy sunny bedroom. I open his drawer and retrieve a white cotton T-shirt. My room now looks like a war zone, shell casings included, thanks to the contents of his survival bag. All that is missing are some dead bodies. This thought strikes me as funny. I could probably call down to the morgue and they could bring some over for me, since we all know each other now, thanks to my meltdown and inability to identify my husband. Apparently this denial is "not uncommon", the words stir me back to reality. What was I saying? I gave my head a shake and realized, later was now, and I had to clean this mess up.

2 GETTING OUT

I do a lousy job of cleaning up. Just the minimum, picking up the staples on the floor, shove the gear back into his survival bag, throw the torn papers into the plastic waste paper basket under his desk, making a mental note to recycle them on garbage day, which is Wednesday, tomorrow. It was good enough, after all, today was going to be a long and probably agonizing day, did I really want to waste my energy on this?

I wonder to myself why the kids haven't appeared during my little tantrum and that is when I notice the faint sound of water running and the hum of their shower radio. Katherine is in the shower (she is the one who always listens to music) and since his room shares a wall with their bathroom, Jordan is probably still asleep, or the shower has drowned out my little fit. "Better get used to being alone old bird" I think to myself.

It wouldn't be long before they would have their own lives and would leave the nest so to speak. Maybe I had a few years but that would go by in a blink. The past 15 seem to have happened overnight. Moving out was all Jordan had talked about since starting high school. He couldn't wait to strike out on his own in his own bachelor pad. As it was now we hardly saw him. He was always out and about with his friends or his girlfriend. Even when he was home he would be holed up in his room with Alexa "watching movies" yeah right. I was 15 once too.

From where I am on the bed the door to my room is to my left and ajar, I can just make out the black nose inching its way back into the room along the floor. "Jesus", I think to myself lifting my body to a sitting position. "He's like a dog with a bone! He is a dog who wants a walk!" I remind myself as a crazy chuckle escapes me. Grabbing the khaki Capris that I had left flung over Steve's office chair the night before, I head into the bathroom to pee and change, then it is out into this beautifully horrible day to pick up dog shit, after all, Buster has been extremely patient with me. I am worried about him becoming incontinent as he gets older so as a result he is walked often, at least twice a day.

Steve's 21st birthday drifts back to me. His dog Boots, the loveable Samoyed Golden Retriever mutt had to be put down days before, and I was the one who had to break the news to Steve. Boots had been diagnosed with Diabetes and I can remember vividly the last time I saw him. It couldn't have been more than a week before he was euthanized. He came running to the front door where Steve and I had just entered, his white fur blowing in the wind he created as he ran, it was almost as if the scene was in slow motion, he was peeing as he went. Steve's mom freaked out as her hall carpet was now drenched in canine urine. Boots with his snowy white face and his tail wagging hard at the sight of us had no clue what had just happened. He had signed his death certificate.

I can remember Boots' earlier days as well. You see I have known Steve, sorry had known him since I was 8 years old, Jesus that was thirty years ago. We were both in Mrs. Lunguard's grade 3 class, something I did not know until years later. Steve had rescued Boots when he was 8 years old. I remember going to Steve's house for some reason, it must have been in a later grade when we became friends, and being amazed because Boots didn't give you a paw, he high-fived! It was ingenious, I didn't have a dog growing up, or any other pet for that matter as you may have guessed. Otherwise that might not have been so impressive. I loved to pet him, he was so soft, and as I mentioned he was white all over except for some tan patches on his back. He loved me too I think, maybe because I paid so much attention to him.

It was in grade 4 and some of 5 that I remember hating Steve. He swears he didn't do it but I have an excellent memory and I know he pulled down my halter top in grade 4. They were all the rage that year. It was orange and made of material that looked like velour. Wow, that sounds snazzy, an eight year old girl in an orange velour tube top, keeping it classy. My mom had made it for me as she did with most of my clothes back then. During afternoon recess one sunny January afternoon Steve had come up behind me and yanked my shirt down to my waist. I was horrified. Luckily most of the kids were too busy skipping or playing foot hockey to notice. So I had time to pull it back into place. I'm not sure why I never told on him, then again I wasn't the tattle tale type. I am surprised I didn't hit him; God knows I would have been justified.

I would go on to hold that grudge though until the middle of grade 5, when his best friend Rick decided he was in love with me and followed me around like a puppy dog. Steve, being Rick's loyal best friend was there with him, unbeknownst to me just as love sick. Through middle school we became good friends, him acting as a go between for guys who liked me or that I was dating. A kind of mediator of sorts, all the while he had the potential to sabotage my relationships, I wonder if he ever did? I doubt it, however a conspiring side to him did come out later in our lives together that sometimes made me uncomfortable.

It doesn't matter now though. He locked into a long term relationship in grade 7 that would span years, include an engagement and then end in a messy split at the tender age of 16. What do you know about life at sixteen? He once told me it just seemed like the next logical step in their relationship. I never understood this relationship, he was in our group of popular kids and she was a skinny little thing with a diva like persona. I never liked her, regarding her as a phony, but I was civil as he was my friend and she was too now by association, whether I liked it or not, maybe I was jealous. I liked the attention he had paid me when we were friends and I wasn't getting it now that she was in the picture.

There was that one time though. In grade 8 he had skipped off school one day to go skiing with his aunt and ended up at my house. Everyone seemed to always end up at my house. He was sun burnt from the snow's reflection on his face and I felt so bad for him that I went to the medicine cabinet and came back with Nivea. I carefully spread it on his pink cheeks and his burnt nose trying desperately not to hurt him. Being in so near proved too much for him because he leaned in and kissed me. It wasn't a passionate, "I want to get in your pants" kind of kiss, it was a tender puppy love kiss; I remember his lips being very soft and he was a good kisser. He had assured me that he and his then girlfriend, yes the long term engaged at 16 one, were on one of their many hiatus', or is it hiatuses? It was weird because kissing him had seemed so natural and comfortable.

He left that night and we lost track of each other for a few years. He had moved at the end of grade 8 and I never got his number, being too preoccupied with other teenage bullshit. We wouldn't see each other again until my last year in high school. He was dating somebody new yet kept on calling me and I ended up going to a party at his house.

It was his birthday and he seemed touched that I had gone to the trouble of getting him a card. I was so disappointed when his girlfriend answered the door, I thought she was very pretty, her long blond hair falling down her back. She had looked at me expectantly as if to say, "What do you want?".

I was very self conscious as there were so many people that I hadn't talked to in a while. They had never really been friends just acquaintances and here I was hanging out at one of their parties. Steve did spend a good portion of the night trying to talk to me but she was hanging off of him the whole time. Saying things like "Steve I need a drink" or "Steve come here I need you." With every passing minute she got uglier and uglier to me. As the night went on it got worse because she was getting intoxicated, sloppy and horny. I started to feel insecure and disappointed so I ended up having a few drinks and then at one point I drove my mom's car to pick up some people for the party, including one of my ex-boyfriends. When my ex saw I was one of the drivers he opted for the other car, I guess he still hated me, I had cheated on him. It was 3 years earlier, let it go!

I probably shouldn't have been driving. I can't even remember the drive that night, just flashes, driving down a long stretch of road I think I may have been weaving, arriving at my exes house and the hurt that he wouldn't get in the car. Not because there was anything between us, I just don't like anyone hating me. Luckily everything was okay and I never did that again. I scolded myself the next day, what the hell was I thinking? I could have killed someone or myself. I was always careful after that and wouldn't drink if I was driving.

Until this point, I hadn't realized that I did have feelings for Steve. Seeing him again had conjured up some long forgotten emotions. I went home that night disheartened, though the next couple of weeks I saw him quite a bit. We even went to the drive-in together one night. I went out that day and bought myself a new outfit, green jeans and a black skin tight turtle neck.

I remember the movie we saw, it was Falling Down starring Michael Douglas. It's about a man who snaps when he becomes disenchanted with society. How ironic as that is how Steve turned out, he believed that we were all enslaved and he wanted to get off of the grid, maybe it was a warning. I flirted endlessly during the movie and even started a popcorn fight with him, he later told me that his mom gave him shit and made him clean up the popcorn as it was her car he had used, but nothing happened between us that night. He was still with Heather and even though he planned to break up with her and didn't have feelings for her anymore, he was not a cheater, he was loyal, it hurt him deeply if anyone was any different to him.

After that night he broke up with Heather and the following weekend invited me to go see his old friend Rick, yes the one that was in love with me throughout middle school, he had moved up north, about two hours from where we lived. I was out picking up some dinner when Steve called with the invitation, by the time I got home he had already left wanting to beat the traffic. Again we lost touch. This time it was only for six months, then, out of the blue, he called me one afternoon and I went to his parent's house where he was house-sitting. From that day on we would be together, till death do us part.

A smile dances across my face as I think back to how shitty that little one bedroom apartment he had down by the lake shore was, that is where he was living when we first got together, very different from his parent's huge house on the edge of the town we grew up in. The apartment was so small you had to sit sideways on the toilet, I kid you not!

The first time I stepped foot in that place it was crawling with fruit flies. He had been staying at his parent's house, looking after Boots while they were away to who knows where, they were never home, and he had left his dirty dishes in the sink causing an infestation that would make the Orkin Man want to run away. I was HORRIFIED! He was okay with it because there was a bedroom where we could close the door and ignore those pesky fruit flies, invoking a protective barrier, as if those little buggers weren't small enough to fly through the cracks of his bedroom door.

There is one thing he did not count on, and that was how I couldn't stand to know what was taking place in the next room. I kept on imagining how it would feel to have their tiny hairy legs crawling up my arms, and hearing the buzzing of their many wings. It still makes me shiver when I think of it.

I lay in his king size waterbed staring at the wall, where he had started to draw a giant full wall sized parrot, don't ask. I later drew a tree for the bird to perch on. I stared at that wall until his breathing took on a rhythmic pattern and I was sure he was asleep. Then I crept into the kitchen and holding my breath, I didn't want them to fly into my mouth or up my nose, I washed those dishes, having to drain the sink twice and run into the other room to breath occasionally. As well as swatting them off my arms when they were brave enough to land on me. There were so many tiny carcasses, my efforts had obliterated that fruit fly colony.

Escaping the clutches of my daydream, looking at myself now in the mirror, to my left, hanging on the bathroom wall I can see a tiny fruit fly. WHAM! My hand comes down squishing the life out of the insect. I will be damned if I would allow what happened in that tiny apartment to happen in my house now. I wash the tiny legs and wings and whatever insides came out of this tiny being down the drain.

Quickly I pee as now I am ready to burst. I pull on my Capris, my T-shirt from my pajamas looks like a regular shirt so I am okay to wear it, after all I'm not going to breakfast with the queen. With a look in the mirror I am ready to walk that poor dog who is now whining at the bathroom door. I do a double take as has been the habit for the last few days. I dyed my hair blond a week earlier and am still not used to it. I find myself looking two or three times at any reflective surface. Anyone watching must think I am a real narcissist, but I'm just not used to it yet.

Steve loved me as a blond. Throughout our lives together I would go through phases of growing out my natural color and then getting bored and feeling washed out from the dark ash blond and bleach it a platinum blond.

Buster is so happy to see me it's as if he thought I was lost forever in the bathroom vortex. He knows what's coming, though he tones it down when he realizes I am not in a playful mood. He can read me like a book. Amazing how something that doesn't speak the same language can totally understand my emotional state. Whenever I am sick he just lies on my bed with me, it is so comforting to have him.

We head down the stairs and Buster races ahead of me, almost knocking me down as he passes, and stands at the front door looking up at me with a look that says, "Come on Payton, let's go."

I have often thought of what my dog would sound like if he could talk. I think he would be a cross between Scooby Doo and Patrick from the cartoon Spongebob Squarepants.

I notice as he looks at me that his eyes have taken on a cloudy look. I have heard that when dogs develop a milky look in their eyes that they are not long for this world. "Hang in there Buster, I don't think I could handle losing

17

anybody else right now."

The thought of having nobody hits me hard and the tears are threatening to return, I shake it off and slip on my navy blue Dr. Scholl's running shoes, if that doesn't say middle age I don't know what does!

Buster sits obediently at my feet waiting to have his leash put on so I oblige him. I had to change to a pronged collar a little while ago because his eyesight seems to be getting bad and he was straining on the leash to go after people, and inanimate objects. The prong collar is the only thing that allows me to have control. I hate using it but he doesn't pull anymore. His red leash hangs on a hook beside the front door, he came with the leash and matching collar when we got him from the shelter at the tender age of one. I sometimes thought of upgrading his accessories but now the leash and collar had sentimental value and I didn't want to throw them away. I have a feeling that a great deal of items are about to get sentimental in my life.

Once the door is open he's outta here! I have to yank him back to lock the door. stupid door always swells and I need to use two hands to get it locked, one to turn the key and the other to pull the door tightly closed. I wonder if it is the weather stripping that is causing this, Steve would have known, he was my handyman and the one who installed the weather stripping. I would have to look it up on the Internet later. So many things that he knew and I would have to now learn. Don't get me wrong, I don't consider myself to be a helpless damsel but there was some information that he just knew, anything techie, that was his field. I had no clue how to set up the Internet or a cell phone. I could hook up a blue ray player to the TV or install a door lock, anything beyond that or if it had to do with computers I left to Steve, he did have a diploma in computer programming and a postgraduate diploma in enterprise database management. He graduated with a 4.0GPA as well as scored in the top percentile on his Oracle certification exams. He never let me forget this important information. Don't ask me what it means, I have no idea, I was proud of him nonetheless. I graduated from college with a 3.7GPA myself, in fairness I was raising two kids at the time.

The sun blazes overhead so I turn my face up towards it and feel the heat, it is wonderful, like being on vacation. The best time the four of us ever had was two years ago, the time we went to Myrtle Beach. It would turn out to be the last time Jordan would go on a family vacation with us. I'm not sure what was so special about that trip but we all had a great time. I think it might have been because I hadn't planned what we were going to do every minute of every day. It was just a relaxing beach vacation. Key word there is relaxing.

Katherine and I rented chairs and an umbrella on the beach and spent the days in the water, occasionally looking for shells. More than once I was on high alert for sharks, I was always afraid of being attacked or having to save one of the kids. I think anyone who grew up during the "Jaws" years has this fear ingrained in them, thank you Steven Spielberg. Mostly we were having fun, breathing the coconut smell of sun screen and the salty sea air.

Jordan and his dad went shopping at Bass Pro, adding to Steve's arsenal of hunting equipment that would never be used. What the hell was he preparing to hunt for anyway with all this crap, elephant?

I did feel safer knowing that we could get by in an emergency, but he overdid it, then, that's Steve, he overdid everything. I would call him the over doer in a sing song voice to poke fun at him whenever I thought he was getting carried away.

He had many hobbies and this year it had been hunting; in the end his heart just wasn't in it. But on the bright side if we ever had a blackout we could get by. Jordan and his dad also hung around and played cards in the hotel.

On other trips, usually to Disney World, I would have to have a plan for our outings as the kids were smaller and Steve didn't like crowds and wasn't too fond of the heat. For instance; one time we went, I took Jordan to the Magic Kingdom in the morning and then we headed back to the hotel for lunch. In the afternoon it was Katherine's turn at the happiest place on earth, by dinner I was exhausted. It was hard to keep everyone happy. I should have realized then that Steve really didn't want to be there, like a trooper he kept going. In Myrtle Beach I said to hell with it and let everyone go their separate ways. That sounds bad but we did spend a lot of time together at meals and shopping, we even went to the movies one afternoon to see Will Farrell hamming it up.

I think the last night was the best time though, Jordan, Katherine and I were all in the pool playing Marco Polo while Steve looked on from the bar relaxing with a cocktail just a few steps away. It was almost like when they were small and wanted to hang out with us. It helped that the pool was deserted except for maybe one other kid, who eventually left, we had it all to ourselves.

The day before Jordan and I had gone to Barefoot Landing and had the chance to hold a baby tiger. You pay 50 bucks or somewhere in that range and you get a cub thrown on your lap as they snap a picture. Steve later posted that photo of me and Jordan with the baby tiger on Facebook with the caption "they have no idea how dangerous this is." I did know as I was reminded when the back claws of the tiger were digging into the flesh of my leg.

It was Myrtle Beach so of course I was wearing shorts, the temperature was probably in the nineties and it was sweltering outside, those poor little tigers must have been boiling in their little fur coats. I had my hand on the back end of the cat and Jordan had the front end holding a bottle that the tiger wrangler stuck in the babies mouth. I pet the fur and it was short and bristly not at all what I had expected. It was more like petting a German Sheppard than a soft downy cat. He must have weighed at least 80 pounds and was 3 feet long lying across both of our laps. There was no damage to my leg where his claws rested but the weight of the animal was a constant reminder for those two minutes that if he had wanted to he could have thrown down the bottle he was drinking out of and slashed my face clean off. I wonder now if there had been a sedative in the bottle he was drinking out of, he did seem a little sleepy but as long as he was calm I was okay.

I wish I could go back there now, just run away and not face what this day had in store for me. Thinking about it reminds me of how I had wanted to return there this coming August; that is not going to happen now.

Buster and I set off for his walk, crossing the street to the grassy boulevard across from our house. There are bushes that he likes to pee on here. Just beyond the bushes is a decorative wrought iron fence that encloses the townhouse community we live in from the outside world, and the 6 lane road, Mavis Rd, which our house faces.

Living here is depressing. It is a rental community, proudly advertised by management with a big sign that lights up and is an electric blue color, which I think reads to the rest of the population "The people here are poor and can't afford to buy a house, so please treat them accordingly" but that could just be me. People are always coming and going, not us though. I couldn't wait for the day when we would move into our dream house far away from here.

Many nights walking the dog I would find myself angry at the fact that there was yet another moving truck, which meant someone else was escaping. You see, living here is like being in purgatory, or is it limbo? It's one of them. Your life is put on hold until you get your shit together and

21

move out. The only thing is time is still ticking by. So your kids are getting older and that dream house you wanted to give them with a backyard and a pool, well, that is getting further out of reach because they are closer to becoming adults. You start to wonder if you will ever get there. Then your husband dies…..and life will never be the same, or the dream it promised to be.

The automated sprinklers come to life scaring the crap out of me and evoking a yelp from Buster. This wasn't going to be a long walk, I had things to do. We have to follow the road and hang a right onto Tiz Road "just a quick jaunt around the block" I say to myself, and move to the roadway to avoid getting soaked. We will have to stop and check the mail, as I have done every morning since moving here 3 years ago. Buster stops and sniffs at some bushes and I stand staring at a tree, I can see through the leaves to its trunk, not because it is bare, this tree is in full bloom, green and lush. I am just so close to it that I can see the network of branches crisscrossing and I inhale the delicious scent of greenery.

A strange feeling comes over me, like I am not myself, it's as if I am watching a movie, then a noise in the higher branches draws me out of my trance. Way up in the tree I can see a red figure twitching. It's a ruby red cardinal singing. I am overwhelmed by this beauty of nature; I haven't seen a cardinal since I was a kid. I feel so overjoyed with the wonder of life that my chest fills and I wonder if I will literally burst. I turn my face again towards the sun and close my eyes. How can life just end? There has to be more. This magical experience full of amazing feelings can't just be temporary can it?

I hear a rumbling overhead and look up at the clear blue sky; an airplane is flying over me. We live on the flight path and everyday hundreds of planes dust us with their toxins, no wonder Steve wanted to leave so bad. Hundreds of passengers are on their way to a sunny destination or arriving home. I am jealous, I wish that I could just disappear, I don't want to deal with this day.

The urge to run surfaces again, this time it is stronger and I have to physically wrap my arms around my body to hold myself for fear of taking flight. The longing to feel the sand between my toes and the ocean water lapping at my feet is almost unbearable. Again tears are threatening but I am determined to not let them appear, I bite the inside of my cheek to stem this flow of emotion. What will happen afterward, what will I do after the funeral? Where is he? It feels like he is here, how can I feel this miracle of life at a moment of tragedy if my kindred spirit no longer exists. Do I believe in God? I believe in something. Not organized religion, maybe reincarnation? That could explain déjà vu. Energy that cannot be destroyed only transformed, isn't that what we are made up of, the same energy that the laws of physics govern? Then some part of us has to live on after our body dies. Steve used to refer to these times of panicked thinking as thought attacks, this one is different, I would usually be riddled with anxiety or have a panic attack but I am calm, maybe I am numb, not sure. You hear people saying when it comes to the loss of a loved one; just one more touch, or kiss, or look. I am greedy, that would never be enough for me.

Buster pulls me back to now and for a few moments, he is walking me. We reach the end of Tiz and turn right again onto Blackbird Street, this is where the mailbox is located. Seriously, who names these streets?

There is nothing in the little box when I arrive but blackness, I reach my hand all the way to the back to make sure, every time I do this a childish fear rises in me like something is going to grab my hand or sever it from the rest of my arm, too many Stephen King novels perhaps.

Mittens our grey tabby cat comes meowing out from

under the big pine tree next to the mailbox. This is where we usually meet her in the morning after she has been hunting all night. This morning she looks a little disheveled, she is not hurt though, which is always a good thing. Over the few years we have had her she has come home with various gashes and scratches, one time she had a patch of hair missing. Meouch!

I close the little grey door satisfied that I am not missing out on any mail and remove my key. Resuming our walk we turn another corner; now on our own street, Retreat Street, the home stretch. There are sometimes two annoying little Chihuahuas at number 21, but the coast is clear today. I am always afraid Buster will step on them because he panics whenever he comes across these little balls of yappy fur, and as a result he hops from foot to foot, the other dog's master just laughs and calls them back to her but of course they never listen.

Buster is not the best when it comes to socializing with other canines but he is great when it comes to our family. In his younger days he would herd the children like cattle, I guess that is his Border Collie half. Whenever the kids were getting in trouble by either Steve or myself he would come and sit in-between us and the child that was being told off at that moment, even though you could tell he didn't want to go against his master he was obligated to protect all of his family members. So there he would sit all sad eyed with his ears down avoiding eye contact with either Steve or myself. Whenever he did this I would yell at him, "Get out of here!" He would skulk off ears further down, if that were possible, and tail between his legs clearly torn at what he should have done. Each time he wouldn't hesitate, he would be back protecting whatever little being happened to be in trouble. Could this be his loyal Labrador side?

Before I know it I am back at number thirteen. Lucky number thirteen, ha, what a joke. All my life I had thought thirteen was good luck for me. It was my number in soccer when I was a kid. I never seemed to have a bad day on the thirteenth, when we moved here we had the option of 13 and 107. Obviously we chose 13. Steve used to say; "you make your own luck." He was not at all superstitious or anything like that. I on the other hand always worry about jinxing myself or others. A habit that borders on OCD; I have to chew my meals the same amount of times on the left side of my mouth as on the right. I have to even out how many cracks I step on when walking on the sidewalk, or else something bad will happen. It works the other way too, if I don't step on any cracks I will win the lottery, that never happens either. Otherwise I would be living somewhere else and maybe Steve wouldn't be dead.

I open the garage door and throw the poop bag into the black two wheeled garbage can that is occupying the space just inside the door, I have to look around to make sure that Mittens isn't sneaking into the garage before pulling the door closed and heading up the three front steps to the porch. Mittens is already there, she ran ahead as she likes to do sometimes. She meows at me like she has been waiting all night. "Oh shut up!" I snap at her and unlocking the door head inside.

3 THE FAMILY

The air conditioning is a welcoming break as I step home through the door. I didn't realize how hot I was until the cool air hit my frying skin. Buster is panting heavily and I know he will need a drink so I make him sit, which he does only after a stern "SIT", and release him from his shackles. He takes off down the ten feet of hallway and disappears to the right into the kitchen, seconds later I can hear him noisily lapping at the water in his bowl. Mental note: I will have to fill his bowl soon there can't possibly be that much water left over from yesterday. I am constantly filling it in the summer.

Mittens sits on the tiles at the front entrance looking me over and with a haughty "Meow" she heads off in the same direction. "If I stopped feeding you, you would die you little bitch!" I think to myself. It doesn't sound like it but I really do like the little feline. She has an almost dog like personality. We got her from the shelter when she was just 8 weeks old. Buster raised her as his own so she fetches, wags her tail when you call her name and likes to go on walks with Buster and I. People who see us think it is very amusing and I always get a lot of; "Is that your cat?" I always respond with, "Yep, she likes to get out and stretch her legs" which is kind of funny considering how little her legs are. I know, I know it's lame. She still looks like a kitten; she didn't grow very big, I think she may have been the runt of her litter.

We ended up with Mittens because our other cat Sherry deserted us when we moved. We only moved a couple of blocks away and I think she preferred the safety of walking along the tops of the fences in our old neighborhood, you see the rental's backyard is not fenced all the way in, we just have two privacy fences on each side but nothing at the back, so she couldn't walk around the new neighborhood from the safety of the fence top like she had back at the old house. Jordan was devastated; he loved Sherry so much.

One of my coworkers found her in the West parking lot of our office building one stormy October day. She brought the soaked emaciated kitten into the office. Nobody could take her and we even went so far as to call the humane society. After talking to the officer who arrived I couldn't bear to give the kitten over to the shelter, they were overrun with cats, so I took her home. She became part of our family and the kids decided to name her after the coworker who found her.

Three months after we moved our old neighbor called to let us know that Sherry was hanging around over there, we managed to catch her and bring her home one more time, back to our new home that is, yet again she didn't like it and by that time we had Mittens, which made things even worse. She had always been the only cat in our house, she didn't mind Buster but seeing that we had replaced her I think really pissed her off. The night before Sherry disappeared for good she slept on my bed, looking back on it now I believe that was her way of saying goodbye. Maybe she felt our stress with the move and just like all of us she wanted to flee.

You see, the move was not something we wanted to do

but something we had to do. Steve and I had been running our own business and when the economy went in the toilet our company started to decline and our debt increased. The only way to somewhat recover was to sell the house, get what little equity we had out and pay off whatever debt we could. We moved to the rental but it wasn't enough we had to file for bankruptcy after trying to carry the remaining debt for six months.

Initially I thought we would be all right and wouldn't have to file, the plan was to stay in a rental for a year and get sorted out but, in the end we did. Let me tell you, that was the hardest decision I have ever had to make in my life. Not only that, the 18 months that followed were almost unbearable and our marriage just barely survived. I think that is a big part of the reason I am so resentful of living here.

I slip my shoes off at the front door, not bothering to undo the laces, and join the animals in the kitchen. "Feeding time at the zoo" I mumble under my breath to no one in particular since no one is there to hear me but the wildlife. I pull out the cat food from one of the bottom kitchen cupboards and Mittens goes ballistic. Meow, meow, meow is all I hear, she keeps going until there is food in her bowl. I put the food away and grab Buster's, filling his bowl but by this time as usual he has disappeared, he doesn't need me anymore. He has gone off to see what the more interesting people are up to. He will be lying in the upstairs hallway outside of the kids' bedroom doors waiting for the children to emerge. Children? Not so much, maybe young adults would be a better description.

Not sure what to do with myself I head into the living room which you can look out onto from the kitchen, open concept don't you just love it. In my opinion that is just a cheap way of making a small space seem bigger, what a negative Nelly I am.

Plunking myself on the chaise portion of the big red sectional couch, I recall the reason for this purchase with a heavy heart. The idea was to have a space where all four of us could enjoy movies or play board games comfortably, since that was all we ever really got up to. That is how it started out but in the last couple of years it had been just me and Steve sprawling on the huge crimson oasis, now I guess it will just be me, I reflect sadly. I grab one of the now off white throw pillows and wonder what we were thinking, a red couch with white throw pillows. At the time we bought it there were two young children and a black dog in our house, those pillows never stood a chance.

Out of the corner of my eye I see the cordless phone flashing. "Uh oh" One of three things is waiting for me behind that blinking red light, 1) my mom or sister inquiring about some inane subject that really doesn't matter and I don't want to discuss, 2) my mother in law ensuring that her son will be properly dressed for his send off or 3) a telemarketer. I have never in my life wished for the possibility of a sales call more than this moment. They don't usually leave messages though do they?

Reluctantly I grab the phone from the charger and press the buttons that will take me into my voicemail. "DAMMIT" I say through clenched teeth into the receiver. It is my only sibling wondering when the service will start. Really, Lisa?! My husband is dead and you can't be bothered to write down when his funeral will take place. You have got to be kidding me. I slam the phone down on the coffee table sending the plastic back flying and allowing the battery to dangle from where it plugs into the handset.

She is so self absorbed, two years older than me, and we couldn't be more different. I was the rebel, the black sheep if you will, Lisa always played it safe. When I moved in with Steve at the tender age of 18 it was scandalous, living together outside of wedlock, how could I do such a thing. My parents were horrified and tried on more than one

29

occasion to bring me home. That could have been the squalor conditions that we were living in now that I think back. My father helped me carry in a microwave one time and to my horror Steve had not done the dishes so the kitchen was covered in dirty dishes and food from the previous night's dinner, my neat freak father was disgusted. When Lisa was in her thirties and moved in with her boyfriend at the time Dan, nobody said anything about it, they were probably glad she was striking out on her own. My parents even helped her move. What did I expect?

When I was pregnant with Jordan at 20 years old and Steve and I had just married, I was told by my mother "don't think you're dumping that kid off on me every weekend" as a result I was always very conscious of leaving the kids over there or taking advantage of their grandparents. At the age of forty when Lisa decided she wanted to have a child deliberately making herself a single parent, my parents volunteered to look after Christopher for her as much as was needed. I guess I can't really begrudge that, she was on her own and that is a huge undertaking even with a spouse. Hmmm...maybe I am over reacting. After all I couldn't possibly be thinking straight, not today anyway.

My world has just been turned upside down. The world will go on as I grieve the loss of my best friend. Lisa didn't kill him, I need to try and rein in my feelings but I know from past experience it is hard not to make it about your personal tragedy.

Maybe I am a bit paranoid but I really feel like I am not in the loop when it comes to my parents and sister, finding out about sick distant relatives months after they are diagnosed, or even their own ailments that may be relevant to my health. At the same time I need to take some responsibility for that. Maybe picking up the phone a little more would solve these issues. I do have my own family to manage, but it is a two way street. I guess in the past they have worked around me but now it is not as flexible with Lisa having a kid. I never realized before.

Part of the problem is I have teenagers and when teenagers give in and say, "Okay, I'll go to grandma's" You jump on it like a lion would a sick antelope. Anyone who has teenagers will tell you the same thing because at this time in their life the world does revolve around them. Well, at least the world of their family.

I retrieve the plastic backing for the phone from the edge of the coffee table and practice gadget surgery, repairing the wounded device and place my latest patient safely back into its cradle. I instantly feel guilty for my internal rant. After all, maybe Lisa wanted an excuse to call and check on me. Maybe she doesn't know how to handle this or what to say. I know that is how I would feel, the difference is I would just call and say, "I don't know what to say."

Something just out of my peripheral view catches my eye above the couch, Steve's painting. It is a large acrylic on canvas creation he painted for me; it resembles a sunset on a maroon sea with Chinese characters floating over the scene, which translate in English to peace. I am always looking for inner peace. My struggle began when my grandfather died and I did not know how to honour him. It is beautiful, and I am taken back to another time when Steve was in his art phase, another one of his hobbies.

We were living in a two bedroom apartment, the one we ended up in after the whole living with his parents fiasco; I can't let my mind go there right now. The kids had to share a room in the little apartment and I remember being very uneasy as we were on the main floor and there was a window in their room, anyone could have broken in and abducted them and our room was what felt like a few hundred yards away on the other side of the apartment. I can't remember if it was me or the kids, either way Steve got an easel, some paints and a Bob Ross book for Christmas that year. He loved it! I think that was the first time I had seen him so excited at Christmas. He usually didn't want anything or we didn't have much money so he got more practical gifts like clothes, occasionally I would buy him something big like one year he got a PlayStation but once he lost interest in it he sold it. It was always hard to buy for him.

The year with the paints was different, his blue eyes seemed to glow and his face lit up. He went on to experiment for a while with the paints and quite a few beautiful pieces came out of it. We have one in our living room, my sister has one in her master bathroom, my mom has one in her spare bedroom and his mom has two I believe in her basement. The easel is still in the basement he kept it all these years later. Maybe he had planned on taking it up again?! I'll never know...

The thought of his blue eyes turn my stomach, I will never look into those eyes again. He had always reminded me of a sad puppy. The dark blue of his eyes accented by the long eyelashes and the way the corners turned down just a little bit made him beautiful. A macabre thought crosses my mind; what happens to eyes when your body decomposes, "NO, no, no, no" I say to myself shaking my head "I don't want to know." I don't want to think of anything happening to those eyes. He's being cremated so I don't need to go there.

Of course there had been a lot going on behind those eyes. His struggle with anxiety; early on in our marriage he ended up in the ER while having panic attacks and was later prescribed Paxil. He was convinced that he had something wrong with his heart. He had gone to a work golf tournament one day and was dehydrated and hungry when he was driving home, as a result panic overtook him. He ended up pulling over to the side of the road and flagged down a car passing by. The poor woman was so terrified by this odd man trying to get help that she only opened her car window a crack and called 911 for him. An ambulance came and took him to the hospital, he stayed overnight and was referred to a cardiologist. They later discovered that he had an irregular heart beat or atrial fibrillation incident. He was a wreck after that, too scared to get his heart racing he didn't want to do anything. The Paxil gave him a life, but he wasn't the same. He seemed angry and was aggressive though without the Paxil he didn't want to leave the house, his behavior bordered on agoraphobia.

It was quite a catch 22 and a burden for him as well as me, he didn't want to do anything or go anywhere for fear of needing emergency medical attention, and when the obligation arose he would lash out causing a fight. Usually in tears I would suck it up and go with the kids to whatever function our presence was required to attend. It wasn't until I got older that I stopped asking and would just assume that he didn't want to go, or more aptly he couldn't. In the early days when he did end up accompanying me somewhere most of the time we would not be speaking by the time we arrived, usually by the end of the night all was forgotten and somewhat forgiven. I was never one to hold a grudge. I learned with time that by not asking I took the pressure off of him and as a result he would attend family functions more willingly, sometimes he actually enjoyed himself. When I now think of the many hours that calculate into days over the years that I didn't speak to him because of some petty argument, it makes me want to vomit. Why did we have to fight?

For a moment my mind plays a trick on me and I can't remember what his voice sounds like. In a panic I have an overwhelming urge to call his cell phone to hear his voicemail greeting and listen to his voice one more time, I act on the urge. I can feel the prickle of tears starting to form as I reach again for the cordless phone beside the couch giving in to my fear and not even thinking about it, I punch in his cell number. "Hi you've reached Steve leave a message and I'll get back to you as soon as possible, BEEP" I can only manage a small voice that squeaks out, "I miss you." The tears start flowing again as I hang up the phone not realizing that no one will ever hear that message, it was a pointless act.

The drone of the shower has stopped and I wipe the tears away, "Have to be strong for them." I scold myself. Memories of the kids with Steve sweep over me: Katherine taking her first steps and collapsing in his arms giggling in her little Osh K'osh overalls with a sunshine yellow shirt underneath. Jordan being flown around on his shoulders like an airplane in his red onesy pajamas after having a bath.

What would they say today about their father? Jordan and Steve had been like oil and water the last couple of years, it seemed that Steve would try too hard to infiltrate his son's gang of friends in order to bond with the boy, or he would be laying down a harsh law that had one time been too much and left Jordan grabbing his shoes and walking out of the house, leaving me in a panic to find him. It later turned out that he had been at the local McDonalds just trying to cool off.

It was the opposite with his daughter, these same past couple of years his tie to Katherine had been stronger than ever. She was enamored with her father and tried very hard to please him. They had found quite a few common interests. In an effort to support Katherine Steve even tried becoming vegan. It didn't last long, he was the son of a Butcher after all, at least he was willing to give it a go for her. Steve taught her how to play the drums when she was interested and bought her some craft items when she showed an interest in woodworking. Worst of all, they had similar personality traits. I was concerned about Katherine having the same kind of issues he had suffered from, there was an edge to Katherine though that Steve didn't have. She was a strong young woman and I felt that she would be all right. I was more afraid of how Katherine was going to hold up under this tragedy. Inevitably this would change both of the kids' lives, as well as mine, no matter how today unfolded.

I could hear the whine of the hairdryer now. Kathy would be drying her lovely chestnut locks. She is a beautiful girl; she has the unique characteristics of dark hair, pale skin and blue eyes. That is one gift that Steve had bestowed upon both of our children, amazing blue eyes. Katherine's stood out because of their size and color, whereas Jordan had inherited the shape and length of eyelashes from his father.

I remember when they were small and Kathy would rub her eyes when she got tired, her eyelashes were longer then, or maybe it was that her face was smaller, and they would get stuck under her upper lid, I would have to pull her lids apart to free the trapped lashes while she screamed bloody murder. Jordan is almost a copy of his father. With some exceptions, he is taller and sometimes, usually when he laughs, I feel he has more of my features. He is also fair like Kathy but has blond hair, and is just as handsome as his father. I can hear the silence of the house again as the hairdryer stops.

It wouldn't be long before she would descend the stairs for breakfast. She always ate breakfast, and is very conscious of what she puts in her body. While other kids her age are stuffing their faces with McDonalds or other processed crap, Kathy is very selective, eating things like Weetabix, nuts, fruit and being a vegetarian absolutely no red meat or pork. She is mostly concerned with cancer fighting foods, probably because we have had a lot of cancer on both sides of the family, the majority contracting the disease because they had smoked, but she didn't need to know that.

The one thing that Kathy lacks is an athletic side, she loves to swim, and this is the only sport she embraces. Jordan on the other hand had played hockey between the ages of eight and fifteen, rides his bike whenever he can, skateboards occasionally, recently discovered a love for water skiing and enjoys snowboarding in the winter. He is also, however, an avid fast food junkie. Although he recently discovered a love for cooking, so maybe that processed garbage will be weeded out of his diet in due time.

My stomach is growling and I realize that I can't remember the last time I ate something. I had seen on TV shows and I remember once at work when a coworkers mother died everyone pitched in and gave her gift certificates for various restaurants. Was that a common thing? Did people forget to eat when someone died or did it just seem like there was no point. I have no idea, nobody around me had ever died, except my grandfather but he was in Scotland so I felt removed from it.

The closest I had ever gotten was when Steve's Nin passed away and he went to England for the funeral, leaving me here to take care of the kids and go to work. That sounds bad, I wanted to go with him but we really couldn't afford it and there is the whole fear of flying issue that I have. I have always felt guilty for not being there. So I never got to see the goings on, not that I have some sick desire to watch people grieve. I just haven't really had much exposure to what happens when someone dies. All I know right now is that if I don't eat something, and fast, I am going to pass out. I will be of no use to anybody if I don't have my belly full.

4 THE MOST IMPORTANT MEAL OF THE DAY

I make the 10 foot trek to the kitchen and open the cupboard that holds the cold cereals. I pick up the most colorful box and jackpot! There are some Froot Loops still inside. How sad is that the highlight of my day is discovering that I can consume some brightly colored sugary rings. It's just too bad that we can't get Boo Berry anymore, that was my favorite cereal growing up, come to think of it they were hard to come by back then as well. I didn't usually eat stuff like that in the morning but occasionally I would treat myself. Steve was the big cereal eater. He would have a bowl as a snack or if he couldn't find something for lunch and I wasn't there to feed him he would settle for a pile of whole grains and milk. He didn't eat the sugary stuff those were all mine.

Seeing him eating a bowl of cereal would make me laugh. He would have one hand curved around the bowl like he was protecting it from some opposing force and the other would have a prison grip on his spoon, you know what I mean? An overhand grip on the spoon, digging into it like it was his first meal in a month. Kathy and I had teased him about how much cereal he crammed into the bowl, occasionally asking for him to have a "human sized bowl" as opposed to the giant ones he poured himself. He always drank the milk, not in the way that some people do, by drinking out of the bowl, he would use his spoon to scoop the milk to his mouth.

He was the only person I had ever known who liked milk so much. One time he had been in the sun all day and sustained a bad sunburn. We went to dinner with my parents and sister that night and he ordered a glass of milk. Then he had another and another, the waitress teased him that if he ordered one more it would be free, I think in the end he drank a total of four large glasses of milk. "I was thirsty" he exclaimed afterward. I wonder if it was free refills? He never seemed to care what other people thought. I loved and hated that about him.

I dig in the cutlery drawer looking for a spoon, what a sad state that drawer is. Mismatched spoons, forks and knives, not sure what happened to the set we got for our wedding but staring at the drawer I am sure that we don't have one matching table setting for the four of us. We have the same problem with plates and bowls, nothing matches and everything is chipped. I know for a fact that every place setting we got for our wedding has broken or chipped and as a result had to be thrown away. We never had much money to indulge in such things usually replacing the items we lost with some cheap crap.

I sit down at the glass table to eat my breakfast of champions, when Katherine appears. She always seems to be able to scare the shit out of me because she is so quiet. I look up at her. She gives me a weak smile and ventures into the same cupboard I had just been exploring, except she comes out with Weetabix. Taking one of the bars, is that what they are?, out of the wrapper she puts it in the bowl she just got out of another cupboard, nope her bowl does not match mine, and she starts chopping up a banana. That's when I realize she is still in her pajamas. "Kathy, didn't I just hear you in the shower?" I ask. "Uh huh" is her response. "Do you not have anything clean to wear?" I question further. She gives a great heaving sigh that causes her shoulders to drop and says, "I don't know what to wear. Nana said I should wear a dress but I don't want to." I look at my youngest child who seems to be carrying such a load over such a stupid and frivolous subject. Ironically when she was a little girl she wore dresses everyday and would not go anywhere without a fancy hat and purse. The purse usually contained bits of Lego or a dismembered Barbie doll depending on what she had been playing with before venturing out.

When she was about five I had taken her to the washroom at Six Flags during a visit and after she had peed her hat fell into the toilet she had just used. She screamed and cried for her hat. I ended up having to fish it out with a plastic bag, then we went to the gift store and bought a new hat, her alabaster skin would have fried without a hat to protect her pretty little head. All the while she insisted that I keep her old urine drenched hat… when she wasn't looking I pitched it. By the time we were home she had forgotten all about the toilet hat.

I soften my voice and say, "Kathy, what would dad want you to do?" she looks me straight in the eye and responds, "he would want me to wear whatever I was comfortable in" her voice cracking on the last two words. I smile at her nodding my head, my eyes filling with tears for what feels like the millionth time that morning and say, "That's right. So you do that. If you want to wear your shorts go ahead, if you want to wear your Chili Peppers shirt, you go ahead, but I will not allow pajamas." A small laugh escapes her and her tears have started to roll trailing down her cheeks, such a contrast to the smile that was now on her face. I wipe the tears and hug her awkwardly across the kitchen table.

The Red Hot Chili Peppers are her favorite band, next to the Foo Fighters. We had gone to see the Chili's concert this past April. It was Kathy's birthday present. I had been full of anxiety at the prospect of going to a concert. After all, the last show I had been to was the '93 Nirvana tour, I can't really remember much other than at that show I had been kicked in my eighteen year old reckless head.

The Chili Pepper's concert turned out to be a lot of fun. They were entertaining and sounded great live, and our seats were awesome! Since then I have started to listen to more of their music at Katherine's prompting. I had heard the occasional song but I wouldn't say I was a fan. I think I enjoy Storm in a Teacup the most. "Whoop de whoop!" It almost sounds like early Peppers but it has that fun atmosphere about it that accompanies so many of their songs. I highly recommend it to my friends and I can see myself escaping more in my mind to their music in the days to come.

It is funny to hear her talk about songs, the other day she said something about True men don't kill coyotes. Instantly I am transported to my room when I was 12 and I am watching these crazy guys jump around with their hair in their faces and the singer is wearing a weird tiger stripped shriners style hat. I did really like the song, but it was more the feeling that I got from it. It made you want to jump around and get crazy too but the punks at school listened to the Chilli Peppers so I never pursued any other songs until they started to get played on the radio.

Kathy sits in the chair to my right and we finish our cereal in silence, knowing that I have relieved her of a huge burden makes me feel good. I'm sure that will be one of the oh so many highlights of today I think sarcastically.

After I finish my meal I pour out the excess, now greenish grey milk and place my bowl and spoon in the dishwasher. Katherine still sat at the table has taken on a hunched over posture and I have an idea of what topic is causing an internal struggle now, this poor child is so tormented by so many little things, the one I think plaguing her now is talking to a crowd. "You know you don't have to speak today ." I say softly to her, acting on my suspicions, "If you don't want to, and you have something to say I can do it for you."

Katherine had always battled with stage fright. Although she was an honor student she had great difficulty with presentations of any kind. Her dad had once told her Drama/Dance teacher that it was against our religion for Katherine to dance. Just to ease her anxiety about school and having to perform in a class she had no interest or desire in pursuing. I remember being horrified that he had done this. "What if they ask our religion, or what if we get found out?" I had fretted like a teenager worried about getting caught in a lie. "What are they going to do?" He answered. He was right. A school wouldn't go against a parent's wishes, certainly not on the topic of religion. I think sometimes I forget that I am an actual adult. I guess one day I will have to stop watching cartoons and eating sugary cereals.

"I do have something that I want to say. Would you read it for me?" she asks turning to face me confirming my earlier thought. "Of course" is my response.

Truth be told I would have been surprised if she didn't have something to say. Steve and Katherine were so close. I always liked to think that I was close with my dad but in truth I am not sure if that really was the case. I considered myself a "daddy's girl" growing up but now I hardly see him. I mean I knew that Lisa and my mom had a special relationship and I liked to convince myself that my dad and I were also in a similar boat. I must admit there were times when Steve and Katherine seemed so close that I felt like a third wheel. Maybe it is a defense mechanism; I wanted to belong so I made up an existence where I did.

When I was about 10 I became obsessed with soccer. My dad being from Scotland had his own addiction to the game so I hounded my parents to let me play. At first I wasn't allowed, "We had missed the registration" or "money was tight" but when my parents saw how tenacious I was they relented and let me play. I was absolutely thrilled. I went to every game and practice and loved every minute of it. My dad came to two games that first year which was a lot for busy parents in the '80's.

I tried to further impress him by trying out for the all star team. I had a terrible try out. I was on defense and went in for a header that connected too high on my head and flew over the back of my head into the net that I was defending. When I was on a breakaway one of the girls on the opposing team yanked me down by my pony tail making me look clumsy and as if I had cracked under the pressure, nobody saw her do it. Needless to say I didn't make the team. I did however get my revenge on that girl, she didn't make the all star team either and we ended up facing off in a game a few weeks later. I ran past her and hauled her down by her hair. It cost me a yellow card but it was worth it!

A couple of years later my dad decided he wanted to coach boys soccer and I wasn't offended, I looked at it as an opportunity, I would go out with him and help him run the practices, warming up the goalie and running drills with the older boys. I could hold my own.

There is a thumping coming down the stairs and it takes me a minute to realize that it is Jordan. "Are you all right?" I call from the kitchen. "Yes, why do you always ask that?" he says strolling into the kitchen. "Because it sounds like you are falling down the stairs." I turn to look at my son. It always amazes me how much he has grown in the last three years. He is now 6ft tall and broad shouldered, wearing his plaid pajama bottoms and a white "wife beater" shirt.

When I think of him I remember him as that eight year old little boy on our first trip to Disney. I can recall as if it were yesterday; Kathy and I were in the hotel room and Jordan and his dad were exploring the hotel. We had stayed at the Animal Kingdom Lodge, what a wonderful place that was. Sitting here now I can almost smell the cedar shingles on the roof baking in the sun. We could see giraffes, zebras and what I think were wildebeest, all outside our hotel window, strolling across a makeshift African Savannah from the safety of our balcony.

I'm not sure what they had been up to but Jordan came back with a nickname that his father had christened him with "Pantshoe". It was something about his pants falling down and his shoe being untied I think. For the rest of that vacation that is what we called him, he also took over the video camera as though he were the great director "Pantshoe" shooting a documentary, narrating our trip. We went to Disney 2 more times after that trip.

The next one was the worst in my opinion; we stayed in one of the value resorts. Not to sound like a snob, but part of what I enjoy about vacation is staying in beautiful hotels. I don't camp, and when I am home I do all the cooking and cleaning, so to me it is not a vacation if I don't feel comfortable in the hotel room. When the kids were small we spent a lot of time in the rooms too, being worn out from walking all day we would retire and watch a movie or order room service. In this case I felt like our room wasn't clean, although that may have been the gaudy dated décor, and there was no formal restaurant just a large hall that was more like a food court. I guess that is why it is on the cheaper side.

The third and final time we went we stayed at the Hilton in Downtown Disney. Beautiful place, I really enjoyed it. There was a hammock that I never got a chance to lie in though, I had been eyeing it from our room. That is the problem with Disney World, there is so much to do that you need to keep going back. I swear they must pump heroin or something in the air as you always have a longing to return. Even now it is years later and I would love to go back again, just one more time and then I swear I can quit. I believe I will go back as I haven't gotten to experience it the way I originally wanted to. What I have always wanted to do is stay in the Contemporary resort, that's the hotel that is shaped like a pyramid and the monorail goes through it. Maybe one day I will go back and take my time wandering around.

For the third time this morning the cereal cupboard door opens and closes. Jordan doesn't find what he is looking for in there so he goes to the next door. Never one for breakfast, I'm surprised that he is up and hungry. He pulls out a box of Pop-Tarts and puts one in the toaster, then turns to face me and Katherine at the table. He looks uncomfortable and awkward. I have noticed that he has been around a lot more lately. I know that recently he had struggled with anxiety about life and death and now he was being forced to face it head on. "You okay?" I try to ask casually, but it sounds stiff and uncomfortable. He just nods and turns back to the toaster. I look at Katherine who is shaking her head at me as if to say, "No he's not." I know he is not, none of us are. "You know you guys, your dad loved you very much, and you need to remember that. Despite whatever bullshit or petty arguing took place, he loved you and he will always be with us in some way." I stop for a minute, I can't believe the drivel coming out of my mouth. "Oh God you guys I'm sorry that sounds like such a cliché, I really don't know what to say or do today, so let's just try to help each other okay?" I look from Katherine, who is nodding, to Jordan who is also nodding. "Good" I say.

Jordan had really been testing his limits lately, in the last few months we had discovered pot in his bedroom. I can distinctly remember watching a movie one night in Kathy's bed when we thought we smelled a skunk. It was warm out and her bedroom window was open while unbeknownst to us Jordan was getting high with his friends in the room next door. Well, I guess it wasn't a skunk after all. He told us he wouldn't do it again and got very upset about the whole ordeal. Steve took him to the doctor and got a specimen jar that was meant to hold a drug test. Whenever we suspected him, the idea was, to spring the test on him. It was hung on the fridge with a magnet for a few months as a reminder. When it seemed to settle down Steve decided to re-establish trust and took the little plastic jar down.

We later found out that Jordan had started smoking again that weekend and kept it up for a while before again we found pot in his room. This time was different though. He had multiple home made bongs under his bed as well as a book he had cut the middle out of to hide his weed in, as if he were in jail or something. I was so disappointed. He didn't think it was a big deal. Seeing all of that does something to you. It's like you want to deny it away because your heart is breaking for your baby yet you are so disgusted you want to call the police. We took his cell phone away from him and told him he was not allowed to hang out with his best friend, who had been supplying Jordan with pot the first time around. And he was cut off, if he wanted money he would have to get a job.

This "friend" had been busted a couple of weeks earlier speeding down a busy road at 4 in the morning. When he realized a cop was following him he headed home. I guess a combination of driving too fast and being an inexperienced driver, he was only 15 at the time, had him over shoot his driveway, rip up his neighbor's sprinkler system and crack the axle of his mom's Volvo SUV causing ten thousand dollars worth of damage. Imagine if Jordan had been with him? They might have done something even more stupid and he could have been killed. Understandably, this was a major cause for concern in our house.

I especially had trouble accepting that Jordan was doing these things. I thought we were close and now I wasn't sure if he was just taking advantage of my love for him to get money for drugs. That hurt. I wanted to help him but he didn't want my help. All he wanted to do was escape reality and I didn't know why, I suspected it had something to do with the afterlife issue, but he wouldn't talk to me.

He didn't have any interest in school and he had quit playing hockey last fall. It was like he didn't do anything anymore. I didn't even know if the drugs went beyond weed. Now with his dad being dead, would the need to escape reality escalate? I wasn't sure. Steve was the one who had initially been suspicious, I was starting to worry if I would see the signs. The enormity of this problem weighed heavy on me.

There is a bloop sound coming from the living room where Steve's 80 gallon saltwater fish tank calls home. I would literally, every time I heard this noise, turn to him and say with a stupid shit eating grin on my face, "Fish fart." Then laugh hysterically. He would reply, "Okay that's enough, it was funny the first time."

"What am I going to do with this thing?" I wonder to myself walking towards it to get a better look. He has different kinds of corals and a few fish, I know they all need to be fed but what and how much I have no idea. I will have to look into that as well, I should really be making a list of these things I need to sort out. "You're going to keep the tank aren't you?" Jordan asks as if reading my mind. I turn towards the sound of his voice and smiling say, "Of course." I resolve myself to the fact that I have to, it had been such a big part of him lately and maybe if I can manage to keep it alive it will be like he is still here. He used to love his tank. Always looking after it with such care at times it was like a full time job.

I sigh turning back to the tank, taking in the sound and the smell. The pumps churn the water constantly giving off a sound of boiling water, and the wave maker has a patterned muted "mwah" sound. Since he built this tank in the main living area, when near it I can't tell if someone is in the shower, there is a constant sound of water running. Occasionally I am convinced that they are but I am never right.

I am half sitting on the back of the sectional, the rear of the couch faces the tank, which is taking up most of the room and starring at the clownfish, who is either dancing for me or he wants to go a few rounds, they are territorial vicious little buggers. I have named him Percy. The technical name of this clownfish is Amphiprion Percula. He did have a partner named Oscar, but he was decapitated in an unfortunate pump accident. Other fish in the tank are a Lemon Peel Angelfish, who I never named as I don't like her, don't ask, we just have some bad blood. A Royal Gramma, that Katherine named Gladys, which is also the name of her 85 year old alter ego, and a Kole Tang that Steve named Nikki Kole Tang, after me.

My maternal grandfather used to call me Nikkicole and ironically he used to take me swimming and was the one who taught me how to dive. They are all so beautiful swimming around the tank, they almost look as if they are flying through the air. I love to swim. When I was younger we had a kidney shaped pool in the backyard and I would be in there from morning till night during the summer. It was my own little paradise. The only time I would stop was to ride my bike to my cousin's house and swim in his pool. I had convinced myself that I could be in the Olympics, I would be the next Victor Davis and I worked tirelessly on my butterfly stroke. Then when I was thirteen my doctor discovered that I had a hole in my eardrum. I suffered through many painful ear infections and then had to have surgery. The surgeon took some skin from my head above my ear and patched the hole, he also put tubes in my ear to help it drain better.

After my surgery I had only been home for a day when Steve came to visit me. Like I said we were friends and he was secretly in love with me in middle school. He said that my stitches looked like the Van Halen symbol. I thought that was funny, can you tell he was a fan? It was nice to be cheered up because I was feeling lousy, and nobody else had come to see me. Worst of all I wasn't allowed to swim and when at last I was again, six weeks later, I had to wear stupid earplugs. The silicone putty ones would hurt because of the pressure that built up and the long ones that were sectioned like a fish skeleton would fall out, and when they stayed in didn't seem to keep my ears dry and I would end up with infections once again.

Any time I swam without anything to protect my ears, which I did on numerous occasions being fed up with my options, I would end up with a horrible infection. It was tough and I realized that my dream of becoming an Olympic athlete was no more.

Oh well, "Do you know what you are wearing today Jordan?" By this time he has scarfed down his Pop-Tart and is busy looking for something else to eat. This kid can eat anything and not put on a pound. I've tried to warn him about what he eats and that diabetes runs in our family, but he is 15 and already knows everything. You know how it goes, we were all like that. He eats around five meals a day, and I don't mean small meals. He has the normal three but he also has his pre-dinner dinner at around 3 or 4 o'clock which can be anything from a Pizza Pocket to a rack of ribs. Then he has his after dinner dinner, which he eats around 10 o'clock or just before bed, that usually consists of the leftovers from dinner. It should actually be called his before bed dinner.

"Yea, my purple and white dress shirt with my black

pants and lime green tie" he manages to sigh out at me. I am impressed he wants to look nice. "Good" I say ending that conversation. "Everyone else is sorted out" I think to myself, "what am I going to wear?" .

I try to take a mental inventory of what is in my closet. Torn between Katherine's approach, comfort, and Jordan's looking nice. I remember a pretty black and white flowered sundress I bought a couple of summers ago and never wore. Steve was with me that day at the mall. We had been vacation shopping just before our trip to Myrtle Beach. I bought the dress on a whim. Thinking that we could go to dinner at a fancy restaurant one night, or at the very least I could wear it to work. It has hung in my closet ever since, it might even have the tags on it still. We never did go for a nice meal on that trip, and I never wore it to work. Not having the guts to show off my pasty legs at the office, especially since lately the varicose veins in the front of my left shin have become more prominent the older I get. Occasionally they hurt, though not enough to be deemed a medical necessity which means if I want them dealt with it is considered an aesthetic procedure. Who has the money for cosmetic surgery? Not me. If I did I would look more like….I don't know.

I am envious of healthy people not those who choose to go under the knife for a quick fix. Is it me or don't they all end up with that common unreal look? Like they are all somehow related. The next time you see someone who has had work done look immediately at a picture of Joan Rivers, or someone where it is glaringly obvious, you'll see what I mean.

Still perched on the back of the couch I am lost in thought when I notice Katherine has appeared at my side. She is as quiet as a ninja. I turn to look at her and she hands me a folded up piece of lined paper. Starring at the paper it dawns on me what this is. "Is this what you want me to read for you?" I ask. She nods in response. "Okay" I say putting my arm around her shoulders guiding her back into the kitchen. Not for any purpose other than to have her with me at that moment.

Jordan has taken a seat at the table and I realize that none of us has sat in the seat that used to be Steve's, more so out of habit than anything else. I withdraw my arm from Katherine and put the piece of paper in my pocket. I will read it once I am on my own before the service. I need to be able to get through it for her so reading it beforehand should take the sting out of the words a little bit for me, I try to convince myself.

"Okay guys, I am going to hop in the shower. The car is coming at 3 so we have to be ready for then." They both nod and Katherine sits down at the table with her brother, who is still eating. I exit the kitchen and head for the stairs feeling like a robot, my limbs extra heavy as I start to go through the motions of a regular day.

5 SHOWERING

Entering my room I am reminded of my earlier temper tantrum. Some of my personal items are still a bit askew. I have always had a bad temper. Steve knew that about me and he also knew how to get a rise out of me. There was one time we rented an apartment on the sixteenth floor of a high-rise building. I hated it there, so did he. On more than one occasion while lying in bed I felt as if I would roll right out the window. I figure it was because we were so high up that when you were lying on the bed or were far enough away from the window all you could see was blue sky, unless you were standing up looking down. I later learned that this is called spatial disparity.

One day we got into a huge fight while living at this apartment; when we were younger and more dramatic you could tell how bad the fight was by how much stuff got broken. That's not true, only the really bad fights ended with some kind of destruction, these occurred in the early days, before the kids. Not sure what the fight was about, I picked up a wooden plant stand we had and threw it at him. Now it sounds like I was super strong or developed Hulk like strength when I would get mad but that is not the case.

I don't know what that stand was made out of but it was very light. It just looked like wood; we probably bought it from Walmart for ten bucks or something. It slammed into the wall totally missing him by a mile and broke into pieces, scattering all over the kitchen floor. My intention was never to hit him, just to throw something, frustrated for not having the ability to communicate properly. That sure got his attention.

One day while living on the 16th floor Steve had come home for lunch and I was there. Just after he left our unit the fire alarm for the entire building went off. He had been in the elevator, when it opened at the lobby he went straight to the stairs and ran the sixteen flights up to our apartment to rescue me; it was technically 32 flights as there were two for each floor. I had been in the unit panicking over how to get our three cats to safety, in the end I knew I had to just go and leave them behind. I didn't have enough carriers and I think they stood a better chance against a fire than having the three of them fight it out in a carrier.

When I opened the door to the stairs there was my hero. He was a little winded and his blond hair was ruffled, nonetheless, there he was unharmed with an urgent look on his face. He grabbed me by the hand and we headed down the stairs to safety. Once outside he asked me, "What were you waiting for?" I sheepishly replied, "I didn't know what to do with the cats." He laughed at me.

Over the past twenty years we have been together if he ever felt that I doubted his love for me, all he would say is "sixteen flights of stairs." I was supposed to take that to mean he risked his life to save mine by running into a burning building for me. That was another one, he would just say, "Burning building" God, how that would infuriate me, especially since he would choose the worst moment to bring it up and I would start laughing not able to be mad anymore. As the years went by my response became "that was a long time ago!" or "what have you done lately?".

It turned out that there had been an actual fire that day, but it was contained to a garbage can in one of the other units which the firefighters swiftly put out, so I was never in any real danger, but he deserves the credit, sixteen flights is a lot of stairs. I don't think I could have done that at the time but I couldn't imagine my life without him either until now.

Entering the closet I find the black and white dress and hook the hanger up over the top of the now opened closet door. I didn't want to leave it on my bed and risk having a layer of cat or dog hair adorn it. I then go to the linen closet in the hall to get a towel. Opening the double doors onto our threadbare linens is depressing, I grab a washed out pink towel with flowers on it. One corner of the towel is actually see through it is so worn out. Things like new towels or bedding never seemed like a priority to me, just like the cutlery and place settings. There was always something more important, the kids needed shoes, or I had to pay for Jordan's hockey, or Katherine's swim registration was due. I tend to think those things are more important than plush towels.

There is a small picture of Steve and I in our very young days on the wall in the hall. It catches my eye causing me to hesitate and look at those kids smiling back at me. Wouldn't it be wonderful to go back and talk to them? Be able to put them on a good path and have them avoid all the bullshit that wastes time. Why is it that we don't listen when we are young? How much easier would life be if each child had someone they would listen to and follow the advice of? Maybe some people do this, but the majority I know and the experience I have had is they don't, we need to learn the hard way. What a shame. This could possibly save Jordan a world of hurt, he has these voices there for him yet refuses to listen to them. I could just shake him.

With the closet door slightly open, I can see a teddy bear sticking out from one of the garbage bags occupying the back of my closet, these bags are meant to be donated to charity. "I should really drop those off", I think to myself. "Maybe I'll drag them out and throw them in the back of the car, that way if I see a drop box I can just get rid of them." I wrestle the three bags out of the closet dragging them to the corner of my room and stuffing the teddy bear further down so that it is no longer in danger of falling out. I can't remember who the bear belonged to or where it came from but it reminds me of a funny dream Steve had.

One morning, Steve was telling me about a dream he had the previous night. His eyes were wide and he was breathing fast, excited about the dream. "There was this bear who could speak. He was looking after this baby, like a nanny or something. The people, I guess they were the parents, figured as long as they left the front door open the bear would be okay and not attack anyone." He finished letting me absorb what he had just said. I sat there mulling it over. "But you can't leave the door open, what about the baby, he might go outside," Steve furrowed his brow, "no, you don't get it, the kid wasn't going anywhere as long as the bear was there. Think about it, who is going to try to snatch a kid who is being looked after by a bear?" His eyebrows went up as if daring me to defy this logic. Like this was the best idea ever and this new form of babysitting should catch on or we are all just idiots! It was almost as if he had forgotten it was just a dream and he was trying to pitch this idea to me. Then he laughed, and said, "isn't that insane! I don't know where that came from." He sometimes got like that about ideas he was passionate about, almost like he was a salesman relying on me to buy into it. Personally I think it is a bad idea. Bears raising children, don't we have enough trouble with people not raising their own kids, now we want to start blaming the bears for the downfall of society. What have bears ever done to us? That was just the way he was, intriguing no matter how ridiculous the thought.

I head into the en suite bathroom for the second time that morning, forgetting again about those charity bags now in the corner of my room. I look in the mirror and don't know who that person staring back is. My face is still red and my eyes are bloodshot to the point of looking painful, my cheeks are blotchy and the dark circles under my eyes have a purplish and black colour to them. One positive thing is the swelling has come down but it is obvious that I have been crying. "Who cares?" I think to myself, "I have been, what kind of person would I be if I hadn't shed a tear."

I lean in to have a closer look, the blotches will probably go away if I can stop crying long enough, but my forehead is more wrinkled than the old guy in the movie "Up". I smooth the skin with my hands trying to make the lines disappear. I thought that I looked closer to 50 than my 37 years. My eyebrows need some attention as little black hairs protrude from every angle and although I had been blessed with fair hair, I have a blond moustache that is over growing my lips at the corners by millimeters. I try to grab the little hairs and twist them into a curl like an evil mastermind would, but of course I am exaggerating and the hairs are minuscule, nonetheless, they are there and I must take care of them.

The hair on my head is limp and lifeless. I am forever at war with my hair. I love to cut it off only to regret my decision a week later, then I hate it and I can't wait for it to grow back. I don't think I have ever maintained a hairstyle in my life. Maybe I have hair ADD. I am never happy with it, when I get frustrated I will chop it off or change the color, I'm forever bored with my look. I like the invigorating feeling of starting fresh, although I don't like the attention that comes with it. After all I am not doing it to impress other people.

Ironically in other aspects of my life I have a lot of difficulty with change. My job for instance, I hate it! I know many people are not happy in their employment, but I deliberately and literally wait for the last minute to leave in the morning because I don't want to be there, sitting in my grey walled cubicle with the stupid air conditioning forever making a horrible droning noise overhead. I have mentioned the noise to the office manager as have others, however the repair man never seems able to get rid of it. Sometimes I think it is just me. I have super sensitive ears and I wonder if maybe they are too sensitive. Occasionally I will be able to block out the constant whining coming from the diffuser, while other times I have to get up and walk away as the sound surrounds me, making it feel almost like it will scream to a fever pitch, causing my ear drums to burst with the frequency.

I take off the T-shirt I had been wearing until this point. My arms were tanned but the bronze stopped at my shoulders, not quite a trucker tan. The rest of me is milk bottle white. My midsection hasn't seen the sun since before children as stretch marks creep up to my belly button with a flame like resemblance. My arms are starting to take on that weird jiggly look that you get while aging and my fat is trying to escape over the top of my Capris. I am so hard on myself. "Who will love you now?" I ask the mirror frowning at my reflection. Steve truly accepted me for who I was and what I looked like. I don't want anyone else. I never did. I had never thought of my life without Steve and could never imagine being with anyone else. I feel so lonely.

I suddenly envision the future, me living with my sister, both of us silver haired old biddies all alone, her blind and me deaf. Arguing over some hard candy, why do old people always love hard candy? Is it just a convenient cliche perpetuated by authors and the media at large? Will I be an old woman eating hard candy hurting my teeth because that's what I think I'm supposed to do?

I take off my Capris and expose the rest of my damaged body. More stretch marks burn up both hips and my legs wobble as I step out of the pants. I exhale and my shoulders round revealing the little belly that I have. In that moment I decide I will get healthier. Even though I work out four times a week I still have a long way to go, and I eat like shit if I'm honest. You can work out as much and as hard as you like but if you keep eating McDonalds and potato chips you will forever be stuck in the body that you are so desperately trying to shed. I want to live a long and fulfilled life. Wait a minute, do I? I always had wanted to but my soul mate is gone. All of those things I want to do I had wanted to do with him. That isn't going to happen now. So do I really want to prolong my life? Maybe I should just end it now and the pain would stop. I could just swallow a bottle of pills, go to sleep and never wake up….What of the kids? How could I put them through that? What a terrible, selfish thing to do. I am instantly ashamed of the fleeting thought. I really don't think I have it in me anyway.

The bathroom is completely white. Everything in it is white, the toilet, white, the sink, white, the bathtub, white even the shower curtain, white. The only exception are the tiles in the shower which are grey, thank God a cheerier color, we wouldn't want people to think that the builders were going for a drab theme. The countertop is also grey. I could just imagine how the planning went down, "Hey Bob, I think we have too much white, should we use another color?" "All right, how about grey?" There are how many colors in the visible spectrum?

My washed out pink towel is a stark contrast to the rest of the room and I hang it on the WHITE, towel rack. At my feet is our electronic scale. I tap it with my foot to make the digital screen come alive, after patiently waiting for it to read all zeros I step on it. It is always a love hate relationship with me and my scale. What I do if I don't like what he has to say is I step on the manual one that lives immediately to his left. Yes, I have two scales in my bathroom, for some reason I have it in my head that occasionally I need a second opinion. I am not even sure what has prompted me to weigh myself today. This could be very bad if I am not happy with the outcome. The numbers stop and flash 155lbs. "Oh" I think to myself, "finally something good." I am down 3 pounds.

It dawns on me, I always weigh myself on Tuesday since I have started working out again, that is why I felt the urge. I wanted to drop 10 pounds for our summer vacation. I feel a pang of sadness as I think I will never escape to a vacation destination with my husband again. How nice that I can be vain on this day that is not in the slightest about me.

Turning back to my vanity I am faced with a countertop covered in two people's toiletries. His cologne, deodorant, shaving cream and toothbrush all gathered in the same spot, I wouldn't say a pile but they are all standing together as if in solidarity against the other bathroom items. I pick up his shaving cream and put it under the sink as I always have, and straighten up his other items so that they are a little neater with all the brand names facing me. OCD!

I pick up the hairbrush, we both used, is that weird? It sounds weird; I don't think that is something you would share with people outside of a relationship. We never shared a toothbrush. For some reason Steve thought that was disgusting, "Gross, I wouldn't do that." I recall him saying at the idea. "Why not you kiss me all the time, it's the same thing." was my response. "It is not!" He disagreed adamantly. I still don't know what the big deal would have been. Its not something I would have done on a regular basis but once doesn't seem like an issue. I am sure many people must feel the same way as Steve about it though as I remember there was a Seinfeld episode where Jerry was grossed out by the idea of using his girlfriend's toothbrush, even just for the night.

I start the shower and take my remaining items of clothing off. The shower feels warm and embracing. I have that feeling of grunge on me. You know that feeling of being outside, sweaty and whatever dirt particles that are flying around in the air stick to your sweaty skin. Most of the time I get this feeling when I mow the lawn, then you have a nice cool shower, and the sweat just slides off of you. That is the feeling I am referring to.

I wash myself and notice how hairy I have become so I decide to shave my legs. I take my Intuition razor and shave my legs and under my arms. Man I love that thing, don't have to worry about lathering up your legs as it has its own soap attached. I shampoo my hair and after rinsing it out I put in the conditioner, then I just stand under the water letting it wash over me. In this moment I am not a widow, or a grieving lover, I am under a waterfall thousands of miles away from my own grief and my worries. Just being in the moment.

One weekend Steve and I rented a hotel room in a little town called Aurora. This was when we were dating. After the apartment on the 16th floor, we both decided to take a break, not from each other, just from being grown ups, we each moved home for a little while and just dated. We got a room with a soaker Jacuzzi tub at the hotel in Aurora, filled it with bubbles and both climbed in. We ordered some wine and Steve was smoking a cigar. It was like we were playing at being rich or something. There are photographs of us in that tub somewhere and we look just bizarre. We enjoyed ourselves for a little while when we moved home, we went on day trips to different places just getting to know each other without the stresses of day to day life.

On another trip we went to Niagara Falls and got one of those cheesy heart shaped Jacuzzi tubs. On our way Steve had stopped to buy condoms and accidentally bought black ones. Now you need to imagine the world's whitest man and then put a black condom on him. Hilarious!

I am not sure how long our move home lasted but Steve's parents ended up kicking him out. There had been a fight with his parents about something and that night he stayed at my parent's house. The next day though my mother said something defending his parents during the altercation, without knowing the whole story, and Steve stormed out. He was now homeless. For a couple of nights he slept at his mom's store, she owned a pet store at the time and he had the keys as he worked for her from time to time.

I stayed the night one night with him at the store and it was kind of fun, of course for me I could just go home at anytime. At the back of the store there was a little office nook with a desk and chair where the paperwork was done. Steve gathered up some large bags of bird seed and dog beds and put them on the floor so we would be comfortable. He had hidden his little black and white TV in the drop tile ceiling during his shift and brought it down for us to watch. The next day we came to the realization that he couldn't go on like this. We wandered around the city with nowhere to go, luckily this was during the summer. That is a horrible feeling, it's as if you are in a race against the sun because once it goes down you need to have shelter and a safe place to sleep. I would never want to be homeless. In the end he asked a former aunt if he could stay in her basement and she said yes. That is where he stayed for a few months, until we ended up in another basement apartment, together again.

I say former aunt as Steve's family is riddled with divorce. Steve's granddad, Cliff, and Nin divorced and his granddad remarried a woman named Sheila. Sheila had two kids of her own from a previous marriage, Stan and Jenny. Stan was married to Breanne, but they got divorced, so you see at one time Breanne was sort of Steve's aunt through marriage but not anymore, that is why I say she was his aunt.

Steve maintained a good relationship with Breanne through the years and we even invited her to our wedding, but later had to withdraw her invitation. Steve's granddad said he would not come if Breanne was attending and a number of others reiterated his feelings. After all she had done for Steve when nobody else would give him a place to stay we had to fuck her over. I felt horrible. These days I would tell Cliff to go fuck himself, but Steve and I were very young and wanted everything to go smoothly for his family at our wedding, so we told Breanne that she couldn't come. She understood as that is the kind of person she is.

It turned out that Cliff, Steve's granddad, had previously hit on Breanne and had been inappropriate on several occasions. Which is not surprising as he is a man of little character. He used to beat Steve's Nin and ultimately ended up leaving her, and the country she lived in, with their five kids.

When Steve's Nin passed, the family found a letter among her possessions that was written by Sheila, Cliff's new spouse, to his Nin, telling her that they couldn't afford to make anymore support payments because money was tight. Meanwhile, Cliff was living the high life as his former battered wife was left to a life of struggle and poverty. She ultimately died of a lung disease while living in a one bedroom government provided apartment, which had no air conditioning. Cliff today is a millionaire and was at the time of her death.

I can hear the water changing and realize too late that someone has flushed the toilet. "JESUS!" I scream as I am scalded by boiling hot water from the shower-head. I was lost in thought staring at the grout freeway running up the walls of the bathroom. A small knock at the door is followed by, "Sorry." Jordan, my own son has just burned me, how could he, it is more of a shock from the drastic water change than anything else. I know that my skin is not going to blister and peel off like a traditional burn would but damn that hurts. "Don't worry about it" I call back getting over the drama in my mind. I am not mad and think, "It's probably time to get out anyway, how long have I been in here?".

Turning off the shower and stepping out I reach for my towel and wrap it around me. Then I pick up my digital sports watch that is lying on the countertop. I have to wipe the steam from it to be able to see the face. 11:47am, wow I was in the shower for over an hour. I can't ever remember taking a shower for that long. I am usually very careful and don't take more than ten minutes, always conscious to conserve water and all that. I towel dry and open the bathroom door allowing the steam to escape, it must look like I am opening the door to a freezing chamber there is so much fog. I turn towards the mirror and decide against wiping it clear, I am just going to give it a few minutes, I then venture into my room embracing the cold rush of the A/C.

6 REMEMBERING

Mittens is curled up in a ball sleeping on my bed and I sit beside her wrapped in my towel with a thousand thoughts and memories running through my head, what do I want to say today? How do you select only a handful of anecdotes from 20 years of life to share with these people? I don't want to share intimate moments between myself and my husband with these virtual strangers. I am not even sure if I will be able to speak, let alone show some vulnerability.

I don't expect a huge turn out as Steve kept to himself and didn't have that many friends, but word of death does strange things to people. For some reason I posted on his Facebook page that he had died, and now I am regretting making that decision. At the moment of his death I wanted to let the world know that he was gone. I needed everyone whose life he had touched to know that he no longer existed. Although I didn't post where the memorial would be, if you really want to find information like that out it isn't that hard now is it?

Ugh, Facebook. A few years earlier we had both discovered how awesome a tool this site was. It gave us a chance to reconnect with friends we hadn't seen or heard from since high-school, and that was great! However, once on there I soon realized how bad it could be as well. When you think about it, there is a reason you are no longer friends with these people. Exes seem to come out of the ether. A few of mine contacted me but I shut them down right away. I wanted to use the site as a way to show off my family, posting pics from our vacations and special events in our lives.

While on Facebook Steve's ex contacted him, the one he had a long term relationship and engagement with at the age of sixteen. It didn't bother me; I am not really a jealous person. Steve wanted to reach out to her as he had become a part of her family when he was younger, after the loss of his Nin he had wanted to get in touch with them and didn't know how, Facebook provided the gateway. Unfortunately, she was under the impression that he was still carrying a torch for her. It had been about seventeen years since he had seen her. He let me read every e-mail that was sent and I couldn't help but wonder how her husband would have felt had he read these e-mails. The one that really stood out for me was when she told Steve that she had tried to be a lesbian, after he had so devastated her that she couldn't be with another man. In the message she actually said, "I'll give you a minute to imagine that." Jeez, girl nobody is imagining you making out with another chick, even in your heyday I'm thinking horse. YUCK!

I had asked Steve later in life why he had been with Alexa for so long and his response was, "I don't know. Maybe it was because I had a lonely childhood and I was more in love with her family. I had to stay with her to keep them.". When Alexa seemed to be getting a little carried away with her Facebook messages Steve ended up wishing her well and closing his account on the social network.

What I know is Steve fell in love with me when he first laid eyes on me. He used to say he saw me on the steps of a portable in grade 3, my blond hair pulled back in a braid; it must have been cold because I was wearing my full length maroon puffy coat and the clouds parted bathing me in a sun beam. I think he might have even heard angels singing. He knew at that moment that I was the girl of his dreams and he was going to spend the rest of his life with me. His pulse sped up, hands were sweaty and he could not gather his nerve to come over and speak to me.

Thirteen years later Steve took me back to that spot, the portable had been removed as this particular style were considered health hazards now, never mind the two years I spent in the same one for grades 4 & 5.

He pulled the old navy blue Honda Accord into the parking lot of the school and said to me, "Come on let's go for a walk." It was Valentine's Day 1996 and there was a lot of snow. "Noooo, it's too cold" I whined. Undeterred he grabbed my hand and said, "Come on." It didn't take long for him to persuade me to leave the warmth of the car. Luckily I have trouble saying no to him. Once we braved the snow and were at the approximate spot where the portable steps would have stood he stopped and turned me toward him and recites the story of when he first saw me.

Honestly I have heard this story so many times I am only half listening. Blond hair in a braid, blah, blah, blah, where is this going? Then I see his hand reach into his coat pocket and pull out a little box that could only hold one thing. I look into his eyes, those eyes that make me melt every time, imploring him to explain what was going on when he says, "Payton, I love you... I want to be with you forever... Will you marry me?" I have no time to think, tears are falling down my frozen cheeks and my head is swimming. "Yes" I gasp. He slips the ring onto my finger, a perfect fit; I don't even look at the ring, I am just in shock, I collapse into his arms. I am clinging to him like he is my life preserver and I am a drowning woman.

I remember thinking at the time that I have never been happier; of course many moments would come along in our lives to rival that happiness. The birth of our children, buying a new home, those days when everything just seems to fall into place, my love for him would grow with each day. We were never the kind of couple who celebrated everything. Many Valentines and anniversaries have come and gone with little attention paid, usually just an exchange of cards. I should have known something was up when he came home with roses that day.

Earlier in the day I had joked to a coworker, "You'll know tomorrow if I get what I want" alluding to the fact I wanted a ring, which I did but I really hadn't expected to get one that night. It had been one of those evenings where it didn't matter what went wrong, we were having a good time. We tried a few restaurants for dinner before going to the school but there was nowhere available, of course there was nowhere available, it was Valentine's Day for God's sake. I was starving so we ended up at a diner where I had a chilli dog and I think Steve had a burger. How romantic! It didn't matter though, and we didn't celebrate a whole lot, I think mostly because we didn't have much money to spend on frills. We just needed each other to survive.

Maybe it was better this way because when he did do something thoughtful it seemed extra special that he thought of me. Even little things like leaving two dollars on my side table for Friday casual day at the office or having cleaned up the house when I had just had a really bad day. We were in love. Eight months after his proposal Jordan arrived.

There are so many inside jokes that I could not explain them all, like "Go left and go left again" spoken in a reggae singing voice. Honestly I can't even remember the meaning of that one but whenever I told him to turn left when we were on our way somewhere without fail he would sing in a reggae style, "Go left and go left again!" That would always bring a smile to my lips. What a stupid thing to do. It is one of those "I guess you had to be there" situations. We all have them with the ones we love.

There was a tender side to him that would want to wake up our sleeping babies after coming home from work, I would plead with him not to, having struggled to get them to their comatose state so that I could have some peace, he would give into my pleas. Even when they got a little bit older and stayed over at a friend's house, all he wanted to do was go and bring his babies home. It never felt right when one of us was not there. I guess we were a very close knit family. I think there is one major difference between us and other families though; we wouldn't force the kids to go to places they didn't want to go, well, during the teenage years. I'm not sure if that is unusual or not.

Steve struggled on a daily basis just to be a normal functioning member of society, all his life what he wanted most was to have his family safe and be able to make us all happy; what many people didn't know was how difficult it was for him just to go out the front door. Suffering from his anxiety for most of the twenty years we had been together, taking his Paxil daily like a good sedated citizen, just to give him some kind of "normal" life.

It wasn't always doom and gloom in our relationship. The same Christmas that we bought the paints for Steve he planned a family ski trip. I couldn't believe that he had organized it all by himself. That sounds a bit condescending but it isn't meant to be, I was just usually the one that would take care of organization, so when he had organized the hotel booking, the ski lessons and meal planning I was really impressed and excited. He had even designed a flyer, I still have it somewhere, probably in a box in the basement with all the other Andrews memorabilia, which he gave to me on Christmas morning. I was so energized and couldn't wait to go.

Once there I think the realization dawned on him that he would have to brave the crowds and possibly ski. Steve started to feel panicked and wasn't comfortable leaving the room so he spent the three days in our hotel room with Kathy, but Jordan and I were able to get out on the slopes. I offered to go home but the trip was paid for and I think he was happy to just chill in the room watching TV. Katherine, being so young, was thrilled to have all of her daddy's attention. That was the first time Jordan skied, he was a natural at six years of age.

After being out one afternoon we brought pizza back to the hotel for dinner and by the time we reached the room the food had gone cold. It was quite a hike from the cafeteria to the hotel. Steve had the idea of using the hair dryer to warm it up, always a problem solver. Who would have thought, there wasn't a microwave in the room. I don't think we ever vacationed again without a microwave and fridge in our room. They come in handy when travelling with kids especially when you have left over pizza so you can heat it up the next day for lunch.

I also took Kathy and Jordan tubing while in the mountains, that was horrifying. They were so little but I wanted Katherine to experience the ski trip and have fun in the snow, I was unable to take her and Jordan skiing at the same time as I wouldn't be able to watch the two of them and there was no way I was letting a six year old or four year old out of my sight in unfamiliar territory.

The tubing hill didn't seem that big from the bottom but once we reached the top and I could see the contrast between my little people and the gigantic hill, I was scared. The workers tied our tubes together and gave us a push. I had hold of one handle on each child's tube and white knuckled it all the way down. The kids squealed with delight as we zoomed and spun down the hill. At one point we slid up one of the walls of the track and I could see over it, that wall was a good 20 feet high and in that panicked moment I thought we were all going over the top because we weren't heavy enough to descend, but we slid back down before that could happen. When we finally reached the bottom the kids grabbed the tubes in a frenzy and dragged them to the lineup, we were going again much to my dismay.

Last year around Christmas we went and cut down our own Christmas tree for the first time. That was good fun and something that I had wanted to do for a long time. It was a clear crisp day, not too cold but from what I remember it was the end of November and we hadn't had a real cold snap yet. We had wandered around amongst the pine, spruce and firs. It smelled wonderful, a combination of the greenery surrounding us and the cool air. It didn't take us long to find our perfect tree, maybe fifteen or twenty minutes. It wasn't like in the movies, there wasn't a spotlight shining down on it as it sat in the field away from the other trees, we just all liked it and I think we were getting tired of looking. After a while all of the trees started to look the same, even though the woman in charge explained to us the difference between the species we couldn't get it right. In the end we got a spruce that didn't look very big until we got it home and it swallowed up the corner of our living room. We had to rearrange the furniture to make it fit.

Jordan had been the one to free the tree from its anchor to the ground. Wielding a saw we were provided with upon our arrival at the farm he made quick work of it. He also dragged the tree back to the barn to be bagged and tied to the roof of our station wagon. Wow, we almost sound like the Griswolds. On the way back to the parking lot we took pictures of him in a triumphant pose over his fallen adversary. He basically put his foot on top of the tree as if it were a kill and flexed his winter coat covered muscles. We all had a great time and planned on doing it again this year. This year I had hoped for this excursion to become a family tradition. That's not happening now, I think to myself bitterly. The thought of a Christmas without him is too much.

When we first had Jordan we didn't have much money. I know I am starting to sound like a broken record with that and who am I kidding when have we ever had much money. So we would load him into his stroller and head over to the local Chapters. We could walk there in 5 minutes, it wasn't far from us at all. It was always so cozy in there, the smell of lattes and espressos emanating from the Starbucks attached to the store, and the overstuffed chairs that dotted the floor made it feel homey. I would take Jordan to the kids section and curl up with him in one of the chairs and we would read Dr. Seuss or Curious George, whatever he had chosen for the evening.

He loved it when I read to him because I would give the characters voices and that entertained him. Steve would wander around the nonfiction section looking for books on whatever hobby he was into at the time. That would be our family Friday night out.

We enjoyed this Friday night ritual for about a year until Katherine came along, we ended up moving around the same time that she arrived. Unfortunately we didn't move close to a Chapters or we may have continued this tradition with our younger offspring. Despite not carrying on the ritual both of our children grew up with a healthy appetite for the written word.

I once had asked Steve what his favorite memories of our life together were. After a minute of thinking about it to my surprise he gave me a list, "The "Pantshoe" thing when we were in Disney, having Jordan, just the whole first time experience of having a child, cuddling with Katherine. Showing off Katherine, remember how she used to wear her little hats and dresses?" he had beamed with pride at me, "I used to love taking her out because people would say how cute she was." I told him my list of the ski trip, cutting down the tree and going to Chapters when Jordan was a baby. "Oh yeah, that was great, how do they make a retail store so cozy? I also enjoyed driving places in the wagon, I just liked driving to our vacation spots but I hated coming home, it always took so long." I interrupted his reverie with, "Oh my God, do you remember R2D2?" The smile that spreads across his face tells me he remembers he looks like a child at Christmas and he laughs his true guttural laugh that was always contagious.

While on one of our drives to Disney we had gone through the mountains of Virginia, one night stopping at a Holiday Inn there, in the morning we noticed a statue across the street, it looked like a guy standing beside R2D2. It seemed a bit weird but I have seen stranger things on TV so I pulled out the video camera and took a little film of our discovery. When I zoomed in though I realized it was not R2D2 but a mining cart with a miner standing next to it. We had a good laugh about that one. After that I think we all had our eyes tested. Why in the hills of Virginia would they have a brass statue in the shape of R2D2?

"Our wedding, that was an awesome time, everybody said how much fun they had." On that note he came over to me and wrapped his arms around me kissing my cheek and inhaling my hair, just holding me for a minute.

We had a good life together, short, but good.

I lie back on my bed letting the deafening silence envelop me. The silence seems so loud I feel the pressure of it pressing on my eardrums. What creates this feeling? I will have to remember and Google it later, another one for the list. My mind wanders and I think of our last argument. Again I let the tears come. The guilt I feel is so overwhelming that I feel like my sobs will suffocate me. It had been about our vacation, he had not wanted to go somewhere hot but I was acting like a spoiled brat. "I feel like I never get a complete break and I really need to get away" I had said to him. Which really is no exaggeration, I literally do everything; I clean the house, make dinner & lunches, the laundry, you name it I do it. "I know but does it have to be Myrtle Beach?" He had asked. Had I really listened I would have heard the desperation in his voice. He was torn with making me unhappy and having to face the heat wave currently underway throughout much of the southern U.S.. He truly believed that making the two day trip was possibly going to kill him.

What I really wanted was to re-create the good time we had on our previous trip, but if I was honest with myself I would realize that would never happen. I just wanted to go to the beach, I didn't want anyone to have to die for it, a kind of relief washes over me that I can now do what I want and go where I like. It may seem selfish but I have lived with the burden of Steve's well being for twenty years and I am now free of it. Even when I would go somewhere without him, which was rare, I would be constantly waiting for that call or text asking when I would be home. It is a stressful existence.

Shame has now started to creep in, how could I feel this way, he is dead, I should be shrouded in misery and wrapped in black cloth. It doesn't mean I didn't love him or that I wouldn't spend my life the same way for another 20 years. I guess we just needed some work, but again, we didn't have the time or resources as we have just been trying to survive.

Music was a large part of his life. I remember the first song I heard him play on the guitar. It was "Over The Hills & Far Away" by Led Zeppelin. I named our first pet after the first line in that song, Lady. If you don't know the song it starts off with "Hey lady, you got the love I need." Steve bought me a little kitten for my birthday when we first started living together. I was terrified, growing up I was never allowed animals, not even a beta fish and those things can live in a puddle, I'm not kidding look it up.

Steve brought in a little wire cage and I couldn't see what was in it. He said, "I got you a ferret." Not wanting to offend him I put a smile on my face but deep down my stomach was churning and I was wondering, "Why in the hell would he get me a ferret? Aren't those things supposed to smell really bad? I had been talking about maybe getting a cat." After a lot of hesitation I allowed him to open the cage and out toddled Lady, our little kitten. She was mostly white with some grey strips on her head and a patch of grey on her back.

At first she was wild, running around attacking anything in her wake. She ambushed the Christmas tree knocking it over a couple of times when it went up a few weeks after her arrival. She eventually settled down, then sadly, about 10 months after getting her we lost her when we moved home during our little dating phase. I wasn't allowed to take her home, my mom still enforces the no pets rule and Steve's mom already had 2 cats, so during this time she went to the pet store Steve's mom owned.

One Sunday morning Carrie, one of the girls who worked there, was opening the store and Lady bolted out through the door into the parking lot. Carrie tried to run after her but Lady was so scared she just kept running away and eventually Carrie just had to leave her and go back to her job. When we put her in the store Lady had started to become very antisocial. Only coming out when I was at the store. She had only been there a couple of weeks while we moved, it seemed like a good idea at the time. I spent many nights out the back of the store shaking a box of her favourite treats hoping she would return. She never did. If I am realistic I think she wouldn't have lasted very long as she was so skittish towards the end. What I like to imagine is that she turned wild and thrived in the field at the back of the store, and if I went back there now she would be all shaggy and saber-toothed.

Recently Steve had mentioned how he was looking forward to getting back to our lives just being about the two of us. I had been as well. Not that I wanted to wish the time with the kids away, they were just becoming more independent and less in need of our time. I even created a list of things that I wanted to do with him. I guess you could consider this my bucket list:

Get healthy
See Paris
Go to Hawaii
RV across the US
See Oldham England (where Steve is from)
Buy a cottage
Buy a boat
Learn to surf
Grow our own vegetables
Retire BE FREE

Unfortunately Steve and I had differing opinions of what we wanted. He wanted a simple existence; I did too, but in a large home, big enough for the kids and in the future grandchildren to stay in comfortably with a pool, tennis court, ice rink in the winter, and a kitchen with all the latest gadgets, not sure if that constitutes a simple existence. I think he would have been happy in a shack, whereas I wanted to be able to accommodate Jordan's and Katherine's possible future families. I wanted to be on a body of water if we were going to end up in cottage country, for him it was more about just being away from the city.

I had some chip on my shoulder, I felt I had sacrificed enough and now wanted to reap the karmic rewards I felt owed to me. It was hard watching other people getting what they wanted when I worked just as hard, if not harder, and yet my dream was always out of reach.

One point of contention though was where we were currently living. He wasn't happy in the city and dreamed of having a place in the country. I was more worried about Jordan possibly running away because he didn't want to move. Katherine was also unhappy in the city. She had become overwhelmed with how many kids attended her high school and yet she seemed to share no interests with any of them. I think for me it was easier to not make a big move and just stay put. The thought of leaving was tempting though, the fresh air, the quiet, I could leave my job, although I would have to get another one, somehow it felt like it would be different. After all if you live in paradise does it really matter if you have to shovel shit every day?

The early days of our relationship, at the time, I thought were like paradise. It only took me 2 weeks to know that I was in love with him. We were in his old bedroom at his parent's house sleeping on a pull out couch as he had taken his bed when he moved out. The room was still decorated as it was when he lived there, the only difference was the pull out couch. The room had streaky black and grey wallpaper that almost had a metallic sheen to it, it screamed teenage angst. I couldn't tell you what the carpet looked like; I think it might have been grey as well. The double doors opened into his closet which he later broke when fighting with his father.

We lay awake in the early morning, not talking just being. I felt so warm and happy intertwined with him. It was like we were the only people alive, it was so quiet. We had no reason to leave, no responsibilities. The blankets were so soft and the sheets smelled of bleach, like hotel sheets. I turned to look into those eyes and my heart and lungs were so full that I felt like I might cry from the sheer joy of my feelings. Then looking into his eyes I said, "I feel a lot of love in this room." He looked down at me and we both started to laugh. He had a loud laugh that was followed by a silly hissing, almost like Ernie from Sesame Street, I used to tease him saying he sounded like Snidely Whiplash's dog Muttley. He brushed the hair off of my cheek and tilting my chin up he kissed me softly on the mouth and said, "I feel a lot of love in this room too." Years later we would bring that up and have a good laugh. It sounds cheesy but it was a beautiful moment. In classic Payton style I made it a joke just in case he didn't feel the same way, I don't know why, I knew at that moment he loved me too.

Those first two weeks in our relationship were, I think, the most fun we have ever had. No responsibilities, nobody telling us what to do. I was on vacation and he was unemployed, we were both too young to really care about the future. We could deal with it when it arrived. During that time he had that crappy sideways sitting on the toilet apartment, but we stayed at his parent's house where he made me dinner and we played house. Then when his parents came home it was time to go and we went to my parent's house because they were on vacation, weird how that worked out.

My sister was being a real bitch, and wouldn't let us stay in the house because she was using it to play house with her boyfriend, so we pitched a tent in the backyard and hung out in there. Steve playing his guitar and the two of us smoking like chimneys. We would later give all of our vices up, except junk food. When she had seen how determined we were to stay at the house Lisa relented and we stayed in the house for a couple of days. After that my war with the fruit flies began and I got to finally see his shitty little sideways sitting on the toilet apartment at the lake shore.

Still lying on the bed I can feel how dry my face is. If I were to smile it might crack and crumble away. The salty tears mixed with the dryness that I always suffer from after a hot shower can no longer go unnoticed. I swing myself up into a sitting position, carefully securing my towel around me, nobody wants to see that, not even me, and head back into the en suite bathroom. The steam has cleared and I can now see my reflection in the mirror. I squirt some moisturizer into my hand from the pump sitting next to the sink and spread it over my ravaged skin.

Not really paying attention I look in the mirror and there it is, every morning when I relieve my face of its dry feeling I would leave behind a vertical line of white cream down the length of my nose, dead centre. I'm not sure how I do it but without fail every morning this paper thin line would happen. Steve used to laugh at me for this little ritual. "Are you gonna get that?" he would tease. At first I didn't know what he was talking about, only realizing after catching a glimpse in the mirror. As time went by that was all he had to say and I would know exactly what he was talking about. I'm not sure how I even do it, it just seems to happen.

I wipe the cream off of my nose with the back of my hand and decide to throw on some comfy clothes, it is only 12pm after all and the car is not coming until 3. I don't want to spill any lunch on my dress. I can be messy at times don't judge me. I also have an undeniable want to look good today. Looking in the mirror I pile my hair loosely on top of my head toying with the idea of wearing my hair up. "Ugh, who am I kidding" I let my hair fall from where it was being held. "I wouldn't even know where to begin with that." The closest I have ever come to putting my hair up is in a spider clip or a pony tail. Don't get me wrong, I have had professionals do it for me, but myself, not a chance. I am just not that type of girl. I am more of a wash and wear, not dry clean only. That being said I settle for a black pair of Capris and my pink shirt that Steve used to call my college girl shirt. It was tight, and I think it made me look healthy and fit to him, the colour showing off the slight tan I had achieved this summer so far.

If our roles were reversed I wonder what he would wear or say about me. He's not a fan of speaking in front of people so I don't know if he would put himself through that. If I am honest I wouldn't want him to, while at the same time I would feel a little short changed. I deserve a send off just like anybody else does. In the end I think he would feel compelled to let people know how much he loved me. Whenever we would fight I used to wish for something to happen to me. I know that sounds twisted, I just wanted him to see how important I was in his life, maybe that was a bit extreme.

I can remember one night we were in the car and we had been arguing about God knows what, probably money, and I was staring out the car window at the black asphalt racing by and for a split second I thought of opening the door spilling my body onto the pavement. Would the impact kill me or a passing car? In my minds eye I could see my body drop to the ground rolling from the speed then being crushed by the dark green Bonneville in the right lane. My hand had even tightened around the handle, but of course I would never do anything like that. It is not in me, and I would never expose my children, who were sitting in the backseat, to something that horrific.

I'm remembering the first visitation I ever attended, I was 18 and it was for a boy that I went to high school with. He had killed himself. To go to the funeral home and see the family in shock, and not really understanding what has happened in that dimly lit room was heart breaking. At eighteen what could have been so bad? He had so much life ahead of him. His girlfriend was crying over his dead body, causing the corpse makeup to run down his cheeks. It was awful. When I stepped up to his coffin all I could think was, "I wonder how he did it?" and "He doesn't really look like a person.".

I tried to shut my eyes so I wouldn't have to look at him

but it creeped me out and I was worried that I would have a panic attack, so I had to keep them open. I looked at the silk lined coffin and his hands instead. He held a sword, I think he was a black belt in Kendo or something; he was a martial arts nut. Once I felt an appropriate amount of time had passed, gazing upon his lifeless body, I moved away and spoke to some people that I knew from school, we could hear the funeral home workers laughing through the door in their office which was next to the viewing room, it seemed like such a rude act, thinking back on it now it was all very surreal.

I have come to the conclusion that I will handle speaking at the funeral as I do with most issues in my life, wing it. "I don't want to sound like I am making a speech and it should sound more natural if I just say what I am thinking at the time." I try to convince myself. What a crock, if I am honest I don't know what to say. Really who knows what the right thing is to say or do. I will not get to say everything that I would want to say anyway, that would take far too long and I'm sure these people don't want to hear it as it would mean nothing to them. As long as I am able to convey how much I loved him and will miss him, that is the main point I want to drive home.

I pick up my discarded clothes and throw them into the laundry sorter in my walk in closet. Not bothering to sort them into the three compartments "I'll do it later" I think to myself. Then I remember the paper Katherine slipped me downstairs and I find my Capris digging in the pocket to retrieve her last message to her father. I unfold the paper and take a deep breath, then read:

"Dad, you once said to me, you don't just love your children, you fall in love with them. We were in love Dad, and though a child should expect to bury her parent, I can't believe the overwhelming grief stirring in the pit of my soul.

I will never get over this loss. Through every event in my life yet to come I will feel the death of the part of my soul that is you. I will miss you until the day I die Dad.

Love you forever and ever. Your pumpkin, peach pie, buttercup. Katherine"

I fold up the paper and hold it to my chest. Steve would call her every cutesy name he could think of but it always seemed to contain: pumpkin, peach pie, buttercup. He claimed that there weren't enough terms of affection for her, so he called her all of them.

7 THE SISTER

From a young age I had looked up to my sister. She was able to do things that I couldn't do and for that I held her up on a pedestal. When I was young I used to do whatever she wanted so that she would hold me in her favor, holding out hope that she would play Barbie's or school with me. On very rare occasions, I am guessing all of these years later it must have been when she was really bored and it was raining outside with all of her friends busy, she would relent and play with me, but the majority of the time I was disappointed by the resounding NO! I would receive when I eagerly asked if she would play with me. Typical sibling bullshit.

One morning after coming back from a sleepover Lisa had in her possession a loot bag. I had no idea what that was and needed desperately to know what mysterious objects were inside the little plastic bag with the handles. She left the bag on the coffee table and went out of the room while I lay on my stomach watching cartoons, curious I went to look at the bag. A silly clown holding balloons that spelled out happy birthday waved at me from the front of the little bag. The bump that occupied the space inside was an odd mound and hinted at a multitude of toys or candies hidden inside.

As I reached out to open it I could hear footsteps coming back to the room so I hurriedly took my place back on the floor as if nothing had happened, sliding my knee along the carpet as I went leaving a throbbing line of carpet rash in its wake. My heart was beating so fast I thought my rapid breathing would betray me and I risked a peak to see who was behind me, it was my mom, she was doing laundry, the laundry room was in the back basement and the only way to access it was to go through our rec room. I let out a sigh as I thought of how close I had come. Lisa skipped back into the room a few seconds later and eyed me suspiciously, so I didn't get another chance.

"Did you touch it?" she asked, her right eyebrow raised in an accusing stare. I looked up at her, "No!" I said adamantly, I hadn't gotten the chance but she didn't have to know that. She then turned the bag upside down emptying the contents onto the table. WOW, there was a full size wafer, a little pack of Smarties a toy plastic plane like you would get out of a Kinder egg and a ring with a pink flower sticking out of the space a gem would usually occupy. I eyed the treasures with wonder and then something amazing happened, she examined the wafer and to my surprise said, "Do you want this?" dangling the goody from her fingers. I didn't even stop to think about it, "oh yeah!" I blurted.

What was I doing? It could have been a trick, by accepting this wafer I could possibly be enslaved to my sister for the rest of my days, and with that she tossed it to me. It was like Christmas had come early. I couldn't remember her sharing anything with me. I wish I could say that I savored every bite of that wafer but I was six and it was a sweet, it was gone in five seconds.

We fought a lot in our younger days, I couldn't tell you what we fought about but I still have the little white scars all over my hands where she would scratch me until I bled. I could never be a hand model. Good thing that wasn't my life long dream. I don't have a lot of memories of being with Lisa when I was young, the thoughts that come to mind are of carefully carrying an almost overflowing bowl of cereal from the kitchen to the living room for her, being a human remote or striking up some deal where I do her chores for a half hour of her precious time.

I do vividly remember one Saturday claiming I was running away, I had my teddy bear in a gym bag and was at the front door. Lisa and I ended up in tears getting worked up about me leaving but in the end I stayed. Wow, do I sound pathetic, most of the time though I was on my own.

I had always thought that Lisa and I were close. During our teen years we were always together, we had the same friends and went to the same places. We were popular and went to a lot of parties. I can still remember the first party I went to. I think I was thirteen and Lisa drank so much that our friend Matt spent the night looking after her. I think he must have liked her because why else would a guy spend the night holding your hair for you so that you don't get puke in it. I had a great time just hanging out and talking to different people and then it got to the point that I had to call my mom to come and get Lisa, she needed to sleep it off. I tried to negotiate walking home with some friends but it was after midnight and without Lisa with me my mom wasn't having it. I was disappointed but looking forward to the next time. From then on we were a package deal, you didn't have one without the other, until she got sick.

When she was sixteen Lisa was diagnosed with Hodgkin's Lymphoma, a form of cancer, made famous by the 90's drama Party of Five, or if you're a sports fan you may recognize this disease as what Mario Lemieux ex-NHLer and former Pittsburgh Penguin was diagnosed with and beat.

She was in stage four of a cancer that attacks the lymph nodes. It was a horrible time, my parents barely spoke to each other, my mom ran herself ragged looking after Lisa and I was pretty much left to my own devices.

I thought that she was going to die. I spent a lot of nights on the phone with friends crying and feeling pretty useless and sorry for myself. People grow tired of hearing it and as a result they dropped off, this was all too real for sixteen year olds to deal with and who can really blame them. I didn't want to deal with it but wasn't allowed that luxury.

When she was sick she had to sleep in my bed. We had both gotten waterbeds and mine had popped the year before so I had gotten a regular bed. Lisa couldn't sleep on her waterbed after her chemotherapy treatment sessions as it made her more sick so she needed to use my bed. This really pissed me off. When we were kids and I had a nightmare sometimes I would go into her room in the hopes that she would take pity on me and let me sleep with her. I was always met with the same answer; you guessed it, "No!" But I was allowed to sleep on her floor. Wow, isn't that nice of her. Now here we were at least 8 years later and the tables had turned but how could I say no. What kind of person would I be if I made a cancer patient sleep on the floor? I didn't even see that as an option.

I guess something like that you never forget, I can remember the day she found a lump in the base of her neck. My parents had both told her not to worry about it, that it was probably just a swollen gland or something. You have to realize she was a hypochondriac at this time as well so there was always something wrong with her and I think my parents were just getting sick of hearing it. When she showed me I told her to go to the doctor. It was a weird place to have a swollen gland and the lump was only on the one side. It didn't seem like a big deal. I was thinking she would go get it checked out and it would be nothing, but our family doctor told my mother to take her straight to the hospital. I didn't know until I got home from school with a friend and my mom took me to the hospital dropping off my visitor at her home on the way.

It turned out that if Lisa hadn't noticed the lump she would have died in another couple of months. She was admitted to the hospital and they did a biopsy and a whole bunch of other tests that day, she would have to start treatment right away that would last 6 months, every other Wednesday and then she would be reassessed at that time.

My dad worked shifts at the Ford plant and my mom, when not at the hospital, worked at a government job so I was left on my own a lot. I started doing everything I could to get attention. I broke the rules at home, missed curfew, went drinking all of the time, smoked like a chimney, snuck out of the house, even went joyriding one night and was almost killed when the driver of the car I was in drove on the wrong side of the street clipping an oncoming car. All of this may not seem like a big deal but keep in mind I was only 14 at the time.

I shouldered the burden and got into fights defending "the sick girl's" honor as teenagers are cruel, especially to a bald 16 year old, and they said a lot of horrible things. I became known as "the girl who's sister has cancer". That I did not like.

As a result I started to hate my sister. It felt like my whole world had been turned upside down and I had no control over it. No longer was I allowed to go out and do what I wanted. Without my older sister there my freedom was limited, as long as we had been together we were free to do virtually whatever we wanted. This is a drastic change when you go from unlimited freedom to curfews and rules. It was a hard pill to swallow for me and being the selfish 14 year old, let's face it who is not selfish at 14, I made my parents' lives that much harder.

Lisa didn't die, she got better. After the 6 months of

treatment she was in remission. The cancer never came back and Steve and I took her out to dinner when at 35 the doctors declared her cancer free. No more blood tests or visits, she was deemed cured after nineteen years.

Our relationship however was never quite the same, it seemed that she had found a greater companion in our mother. And once again I found myself alone.

Life goes on as it always does. I found Steve and we married, had the kids and I drifted from my family, sometimes being excluded and not always being aware of it. As I realized one Christmas my mom, sister and aunt were going to see Miss Saigon in the city, they chatted excitedly about it disregarding the fact that I was sitting there being left out. They planned it all in front of me and never even considered asking me to go. I mean it was common knowledge that I didn't have the money but I would have politely declined, all I wanted was to be included. Maybe they were trying to spare me the embarrassment. But by then it was more than apparent that I was the black sheep of the family and they were just treating me as such.

They were probably worried that I would show up in jeans and a t-shirt to the theatre but I wouldn't have done that. The more I thought about my life the more I realize that I was an outsider even before cancer entered our home. I was criticized by extended members of our family for how I acted, how I dressed and for not following what was deemed by the rest of the family as the rules of society. I was just a rebellious teen that needed to navigate her way through the bumpy road of adolescence, which was complicated further by my sibling's illness.

This treatment didn't end when I left home and moved in with Steve at 18. It didn't even end when I married him 3 years later or even after Katherine was born, as a matter of fact I feel like I am still treated like an outsider by my family and that scares me, as once again I am alone in my life. It is really easy to blame other people and shirk any responsibility right now. I have to realize that my sister didn't move out of the house until she was almost thirty, so it would make sense for her to be closer, whereas I would come by to get fed or attend an event. Weeks could go by without any of them hearing from me. I am not truly alone like before, I have my children who embrace me being in their lives and would never dream of leaving me out of anything, and that is what is important to me now. I do hope that I can be accepted back to the fold though. It still hurts being treated like that. I don't understand it and I'm not sure if maybe they feel that I have done something to offend them.

When Lisa decided to try in vitro fertilization to become a single mother at 40 I was supportive. She went through with the procedure and Christopher was due to arrive the following January.

Naturally being her only sister and since she had thrown my baby shower 15 years earlier I had assumed that it would make sense for me to handle the details. When the subject was brought up with Lisa in the second week of October, 2 months before the intended birth, she told me that the room had already been booked by our mother and her best friend would be sending out the invitations. I had mixed emotions, hurt and relieved. Hurt because she was my only sister and had assumed the role of shower giver for me, but relieved that I didn't have to throw the party. It didn't take away from my excitement of the arrival of my nephew. I showed up early to help with the decorations and helped where I could. As it happened Steve got to build the nursery for Christopher and in the end I helped with the painting and little tasks that I could accomplish.

Once my nephew was born Steve kept on talking about who would be the God parents. I didn't want to hear him; he didn't want to be chosen but was also convinced that we wouldn't be asked. Again I was having mixed feelings. How do you tell someone that you don't want that honour? I had raised my kids and was ready to move on to the next phase of my life. I had resolved myself to the fact that I didn't want the responsibility, my kids are almost grown and I was thinking of Steve and I starting our lives over just the two of us but, like Miss Saigon, I wanted to be asked.

One fateful night Lisa called me and told me that she had chosen her friend Camille to be the Godmother, it didn't hurt as much as I thought it would probably because Steve and I had been talking about it for months before. When she informed me I told her, "I am glad, I wasn't sure how to let you know but I don't want to raise Christopher. Steve and I are almost finished raising Jordan and Katherine and we are just about to enter a new chapter in our lives where it is just the two of us." She was quiet for a little while then said, "okay, Camille was worried that you may be upset so she wanted me to make sure that I told you.", "No, I'm not upset, relieved." That was the truth, and with that the subject was closed.

8 THE LAST DAY

Thinking about Steve's last day on this planet, it almost seemed like he knew. I know that sounds crazy, but he wasn't on his computer all day, that is unusual, and he hung out with all of us individually.

He had spent the morning with Katherine in her room. I just left them because sometimes they have "real talks" as the kids say. They share a similar belief system and some of their ideas are, let's say, unique. I could hear them laughing and at one point there was a loud ruckus coming from the room, but they were having fun and for once I didn't want to be the wet blanket, so I left them to it.

After lunch he ventured into Jordan's room and played Xbox and chatted with his son, something he hadn't done in a long time. Probably not since Jordan was 9 or 10. Once Jordan was able to beat Steve at video games he was done. No, once he started to act as his own man, that's when they seemed to part. So naturally I wasn't going to interfere with this male bonding with my petty requests for dishes and laundry, it seemed okay to leave it for later today. Did I know too somehow?

After dinner it was my turn, we cuddled on the couch

watching the TV. I was lying with my back to him and he held me tight and started to kiss my neck. I won't get into the passionate details but we enjoyed our time together. He told me how much he loved me and we talked about the future.

"I think we should move in a couple of years" he said. I was surprised as we had talked about moving on and off since we came to the rental, but we had not decided when or where we would be going. "Okay" I said to him and he seemed just as surprised that I was agreeing having always been the one that wanted to stay put. I only wanted that so that the kids could continue on having some kind of constant in their lives. "Where should we go?" The question hung between us for a little while until, "why don't we do some research and go from there" was his response. I was content with that. I think we both started to want the same basic thing, a house with some land to have our own veggie garden. And to get out of the city! That was the most important thing.

He started to get up and said, "I'm going to go to the liquor store. Do you want anything?" I give him a smirk as he knows I am not a drinker, although occasionally I will indulge. It was only 8pm the night is still young so maybe we can watch a movie and eat popcorn when he returned. "No thanks, but hurry back I am getting tired and I want to watch a movie" was my response. I don't feel like I have had a weekend unless we do the ritual of watching a movie on Saturday night. I watched him walk down the hall, putting his sweater on he hesitates and changing his mind he hangs the hoodie back on the hook at the front door, he is swinging his keys and it struck me, "I usually go to the store not Steve. I wonder why he didn't ask me to go." At the time I just brushed it off although now I haven't figured out if I feel guilty for not going instead of him, what is that called? I think I remember hearing the term survivor guilt. Is that it? Maybe he wouldn't have died if I had gone or maybe this was inevitable.

Just before we sold the house our lives were in a shambles and we were in debt over $150,000, $500,000 if you include the house. That can take a real toll on your psychological well being. Steve had suffered from depression periodically before our mountain of debt had accumulated. On more than one occasion I know he had contemplated suicide. When you are desperate and feel like you are never going to recover, unrealistic thoughts tend to bounce around in your head.

One night while lazing around on the big red couch, it sounds like a children's television show, he had said to me in a very stern voice, "listen to me… if something happens, I mean, if I die and anything about it seems questionable just forget it, don't force an investigation, don't demand an autopsy, in fact, tell them I am Muslim and that no autopsy is to be performed, just move on." I looked at him confused, "What are you talking about?" I had asked at the preposterous comment. He took a hold of both of my arms pulling me to a sitting position so that he could look me in the face and lightly squeezed my limbs; he took a deep heaving sigh and said, "If things get too bad I want out." My face fell. "Don't get upset. I just can't handle this the way you can. You have to understand this is a last resort, but if I'm not able to climb out of this pit I am in and it just keeps getting deeper I don't want to be around anymore." My mouth opens to protest everything that he has just said but he holds up his hand to stop me from talking and goes on, "I will make it look like an accident, then you can still get the insurance money. You will be okay." The fact that he was even considering this as an option is beyond me. A million thoughts run through my head, Katherine not being walked down the aisle at her wedding by her father, Jordan's kids not knowing his dad. "WHAT THE HELL ARE YOU TALKING ABOUT?!" I roar at him. "Don't say things like that. That is the most selfish thing I have ever heard. NOBODY is going ANYWHERE!" He looked into my face with those puppy eyes and drew me in for a hug. I pushed against him and walked into the kitchen to complete any menial task needing to be done just to get away from the situation.

The conversation was over and I didn't want to be around him as that would mean having to talk some more about his ridiculous plan. First, how dare he make that decision for all of us, we are a family and willingly offing yourself because life gets tough is not the answer! He is talking about deserting his family forever. We were supposed to grow old together, and had just recently started to reminisce about the early days and getting back to it just being the two of us. Second, I mean, I have watched CSI, I know what kind of technology you are up against, that would never work. It was crazy talk and I was not going to put up with that!

You have to admire people who live their lives and say they have no regrets, admiration or disbelief because maybe they are just big liars. I don't think Steve would be happy about dying so young. I know I wouldn't be. Now I just have to do what I can to live a long life for my children. I wonder how his death will affect my future, it really can only go one of two ways; I will either become a hermit and shut myself away from the world, decaying with each passing day until I meet my end, wow, that sounds cheery, or, I can take this as motivation to live my life to the fullest.

A small part of me is relieved to have him gone. I don't have that anxiety I mentioned before of being at a social gathering and worrying if he is okay, wondering if he is nudging me because he wants to leave. I can vacation wherever the hell I like, the hotter the better, and not have to worry about the heat or what he is doing, or if he is having fun. That load is gone and a weight has been lifted off of me. No more of his snoring in the middle of the night jolting me awake, or the way he would rip his nose hairs out anywhere, that was embarrassing, whether people could see him or not. It was easy to mistake him for picking his nose as he used to pinch the hair between his fingernails and yank them out using the nails as if they were tweezers. At the same time this means he is also gone, and I would gladly put up with another 20 years of these silly habits to have him back.

One of my greatest fears is depending on someone else to look after me. If I were to get sick or when I'm older if I can't look after myself, I know I am a control freak but I worry about being a burden on others. I used to worry about getting cancer or something and Steve would have to take care of me. You know what I was afraid of? The toll it would take on him, and the state the house would be in.

Jesus, what is wrong with me. Who cares about that shit? Well, I guess I do. I can't relax in a messy place. Another of my top ten fears is being alone. I get to face both of these at the same time, lucky me! Not that I am sick, I just get to worry about who will take care of me as I get older and the possibility of being elderly and on my own is a very distinct chance now, maybe I can guilt Katherine into staying with me, hmmm. Oh please I would never do that to her, I know I could, but she needs to have a life. It is going to be hard enough for her to strike out on her own, she doesn't need me holding her back. My other fears are heights, enclosed spaces, dying, confrontation and the list goes on and on.

At the funeral home the other day I requested a closed casket as I want to remember my husband full of life, not stiff and grey. Katherine had a private viewing of him and she seemed to be okay with it. Before seeing him I had warned her that he may not look like himself. She didn't want anyone to go with her. She just wanted to spend a few last minutes with her dad. I waited for her in the office just in case she needed me. She had agreed that he did look different but it was closure that she had needed.

I am having a hard time knowing how to deal with Katherine. I don't like the way that sounds, her dad was always cuddly and soft with her as she suffered some of the same afflictions that Steve did. I on the other hand am a different person, I like the hugs but I am a busy woman and don't always stop for the embraces that I should, there is always a meal to make, a toilet to clean or a dog to walk. I don't think her anxieties are to the same degree as Steve's were, but they are present and sometimes I find it incredibly frustrating when she is having trouble dealing with her fears. Whether it is presenting in front of her class or she is excessively upset because her brother touched her clean bowl that she was going to pour pretzels into. Who cares! If you get the presentation over with then you can relax, and your brother isn't that dirty, the bowl is fine.

These "issues" seem like trivial things to me, but I know they are like life and death trials for her and I worry how she will survive as an adult. Don't get me wrong, she is not always like this, there is a temper that smoulders under her sweet exterior and I am sure that nobody will mess with her, but when she gets this way she just seems so vulnerable and that scares me.

I recall when I was younger we had a friend of the family who died, we called him big Bill Hold, he was over 6 feet tall and probably 260 pounds with a very broad build, in short he was a big guy. When he died he was in his seventies and I was twenty-five, I purposely did not go to the visitation because I didn't want to see him crammed into a box like a sardine. My aunt told me that they would be closing the casket before the funeral so I waited and went to the service just as it was supposed to begin, but when I arrived at the church I didn't know where to go and

I opened the wrong door, there he was. Just as I had feared, spilling out of the coffin, he looked like a man in a poorly fitted suit, his chest rising out of the coffin a good 6 inches, he didn't look like he was sleeping, he looked as though he was attempting a Houdini trick, or like someone had used a shoe horn to wedge him into the Oak box. I was so upset that I cried like a baby throughout the whole ceremony. I'm sure some members of his family were wondering who this inconsolable girl was. I haven't been to another funeral since.

After I requested the closed casket the funeral home asked me multiple times about opening it, I declined each time to the point of annoyance and in the end I snapped saying, "What part of close the fucking lid don't you understand?" I immediately regretted my little outburst. "It is just that this is the way some family members need to say goodbye" a wounded sales woman responds. "Listen" I say drawing up all of my courage while at the same time softening my voice resentful of the forced confrontation. "I don't want to remember him like that. I want the casket closed and that is that." She nods and that tells me I have finally gotten my point across and I won't be asked again. I am proud of myself for a fleeting moment as confrontation is one of my fears. Steve would have been so proud. Pride is an emotion I rarely feel in myself, but I stood my ground and it would seem I got my way, but then paranoia sets in and I wonder if someone has contacted her regarding this issue. Someone might have felt it is improper to have a closed casket when the person didn't suffer a horrible disfiguring death. Well, forget that! This day is about what Steve wanted and I intend to honour his wishes.

Note to self I need to go and talk to someone about the rage I am currently struggling with. Now with Steve gone I am not sure if I can keep a level head, he is not here to make all of these big decisions. At any rate I am glad I have dealt with this because if I had to deal with this matter today I am so drained that I would just let anyone do whatever they want.

The exhaustion is unbelievable. There is no fight left in me.

The doorbell rings, I grab the T-shirt and jeans and head downstairs. Opening the front door on a man maybe mid thirties wearing a suit. His top lip is beaded in sweat. I look at him expectantly, "Mrs. Andrews? I am from Turner's funeral home." I nod in response and hand him the clothes. "Thank you ma'am." He says and turns to leave. "I'll ma'am you, little punk" I seethe, there is nothing worse than being called that, it makes me feel my age. I close the door and head back upstairs.

9 RETROSPECTIVE INTROSPECT

A good portion of my life feels like a lie, I wanted to be an outdoorsy athletic person so that is how I portray myself. Really most weekends I sit on the couch watching TV and eating junk food rotting away. The funny thing is I don't think I am fooling anyone. While at work most of my discussions with other employees involve recapping the latest TV show. Come to think of it that seems to be a main point of conversation when I am with my parents and sister as well. When that topic has been exhausted we move on to the latest movies that we have seen and I am not talking about new releases at the theatres, this is On Demand/Netflix stuff.

Let's face it a slightly overweight middle aged woman who only talks about TV and the latest marathon she has watched on Netflix isn't doing a whole lot of hiking. I have ski boots in my closet that have never been used and I have only been skiing maybe 5 times in my life. But in my mind I am a skier. I build it up every year when the snow comes that I am going skiing on a regular basis, I would love to but I can't afford it. I don't even know if that is the truth because a small part of me is afraid, I don't want to get hurt and I suffer from acrophobia, fear of heights.

This year I had asked for ski lessons because I really think that I would like to live that fantasy life I have built up in my mind. In the fantasy I am lean and solid, an avid runner who loves to be outside regardless of the weather. My sport repertoire would include of course running, downhill skiing as well as cross country, hiking, kayaking, basically the ability to do anything. I would own a chalet and spend most of my time there out of the city. In reality I workout but like to eat junk food. If I didn't work out I would probably be 300 pounds. While at the same time if I gave up the junk food I would probably be the lean machine I fantasize about. I am naturally athletic but I think my endurance would be pretty bad if I tried to just go running right now.

Katherine has been a good influence on me since she has a love bordering on obsession with swimming, she drags me along with her to the pool. I pretend like it's a chore and it does feel that way until I am in the water then I am always glad that I came. We had been talking about taking Kayak lessons. I think that I need to do less talking and more doing. I wonder if most people feel this way about their lives.

I like to play a game with myself, what would I do if I won the lottery? Throughout my life obviously this has changed with my situations. Most recently if I won the lottery I would buy a detached house in the city, it would probably not be too much, just a cookie cutter house on one of the quieter streets with an adequate yard and enough room for the four of us. My blue Porsche Boxter convertible would be in the garage along with the family Volvo for the colder months, and I think Steve would have had some kind of Mercedes sedan. He liked big cars that I teasingly referred to as old man cars. But I would also buy a plot of land in the country on a lake where I would have a custom built chalet/cottage with a HUGE stone fireplace, I mean one that you could walk into like you would find in a castle. Open concept, which works for the chalet/cottage look, so that when you walked through the double doors you could see into the living room where the giant fireplace was. Hardwood throughout except on the upper level, which would be carpeted and so would the bedrooms on the second floor. And I mean plush beautiful carpet that you can see the vacuum lines in after it had been cleaned. The stairs would be in the middle of the hallway leading up to a walkway that led off in both directions to the sleeping quarters and enough bedrooms to sleep ten people, future grandchildren! The kitchen would be state of the art with a centre island and a pantry, and a big table in a rounded nook that is surrounded by windows that face the lake.

We would have a lot of land and a pool in the backyard, during the winter we would put an enclosure around the pool so that it could be used year round. A three car garage would be attached to the house by a corridor and housed in this separate building would be all kinds of toys, a jeep, some ATV's, snowmobiles, kayaks, paddle boats, and whatever else I could think of. So no matter who is at the cottage there is something for everyone to do.

Lastly I would have a secret passage way, for the winter to get out to the pool. That way you wouldn't have to go outside in the cold. The whole building would be run by renewable energy, solar panels, a wind mill, geothermal, we would be off the grid even the cars if possible would be bio-diesel. It would be awesome. Steve would have loved it except he would want a boat, well I guess we could do that as we are right on a lake. In the winter it would join the toys in the garage.

We knew a couple that had a boat. I have no idea what kind of a vessel it was, to me I would have called it a speed boat as it was sleek and had a long body with a pointy nose. There were two seats up front and a bench seat that ran the width of the boat where the four of us sat. Under the nose there was also a sleeping compartment with a bed in it. The guy was actually a boat mechanic so he had full access to a marina and he was able to buy old boats and fix them up. We had gone out on the water a few times and it was so nice. We actually used the boat instead of a car to go out for dinner, now that was a unique experience pulling up at a dock outside Boston Pizza and getting out of a boat. Being a city girl I was worried about someone stealing it but our friends just laughed at me and tied it up. While heading home in the boat from the restaurant Steve seemed so happy and relaxed, we sat back on the big bench seat, his arm around me, we were grinning like a couple of idiots.

I feel like the worst is yet to come. It is almost like I have been in denial as if I am pretending he is away or something and the more time that goes by the worse I will miss him. The familiar prickly feeling has returned to my eyes, will it ever go away. Will it ever be possible to remember something about him without tears coming to my eyes? I know it has only been a few days but this is one of those instances where it feels as though that feeling will never end. Like when your children are babies and have colic, you are so sleep deprived that you regret having kids because you didn't know that this is what it would be like. Then a week later your baby is sleeping through the night and fast forward sixteen years that bout of colic is just a blip in your rearview mirror. At the time you feel stuck in it that is how I feel now.

I loved him more than I thought was possible to love a man. He was a good man and we were happy together. Removing all of the day to day crap we just wanted to be silly together. He once built a Stonehenge arch out of toilet paper rolls while occupying the bathroom knowing that I would be the next one to use that room and it would make me laugh. It did. I never lost the feeling of excitement as my work day would come to a close knowing that I would soon be with him again. He helped me to be affectionate and unselfish.

When he had his motorcycle we would go to the farmer's market and get fresh fruit just for something to do together. We dropped by my mom and dad's on his bike and he talked my mom into getting on the back as she had never been on a bike before. Steve wasn't about to let her go through life without having the thrill of a motorcycle ride. She loved it and I think she appreciated that he did that for her. When her ride was over she struggled to remove my helmet but was laughing the whole time and once finally free she said, "well I can cross that off my bucket list." I think he had a fear of regret and that's why he took on so many hobbies.

We got our gun licenses together one weekend just the two of us and even went out to the range. It turned out I was a pretty good shot. Before we did that I was afraid of guns and even during the course I was a little apprehensive but once I started handling the firearms the fear went away. He gave me confidence in myself and always told me what a good person, mother and wife I was. We had a good life together and in truth I wouldn't change anything because if I did then the good times might not have been so good.

I sit down at his desk, abandoning my earlier thought of winging it, I open his MacBook and start to type:

Eulogy

Steve was a good man, he was loved by his family.

He would negotiate hugs from Jordan and take all that Katherine had to give because she gave them away for free. He was sensitive and vulnerable under his tough outer exterior. I know when we fought it hurt him as much as it did me. We truly were soul mates joined by a bond that I cannot explain, devoted to each other with every bit of our hearts.

He loved music and was an accomplished guitar player as well as drummer. Unfortunately the real world got in the way and he had to periodically put this hobby on the shelf. But he never forgot about it. He threw himself into everything, whether it was building a model rocket with Jordan in first grade, providing for his family or getting Katherine to see her favorite band.

I knew him for most of my life and I am a better person because of him. I honestly can't say where I would have been without him or him without me. We are a matching pair, a package deal, a combo #4 at Wendy's. What will I do without him?

I stop typing and have a sudden panicked thought to myself, "is the spouse supposed to give a eulogy?" Having had no real experience with this sort of thing I am unsure while at the same time I really don't care about tradition and neither did Steve, he is being dressed in a t-shirt and jeans for Christ's sake.

At our wedding he had two best men, everyone and I mean everyone, tried to talk him out of it but he wanted both Tony and Rick to stand up for him and that is what they did. It was a little ridiculous how people can be. I can still remember the jeers of, "you can't have two best men!" and "what do you think you're doing?" On the day it was fine there was no catastrophic disaster, God didn't strike him down, the only time it was a problem was when it came to signing the registry but Tony was okay to step aside and let Rick take care of that. Rick did later return the favour at his wedding, asking Steve to be his best man and Tony having a brother asked Steve to be a groomsman for his special day, so it was nice for everyone.

"Fuck it" I think to myself. "He would have wanted me to buck the tradition at a time like this."

10 THE OUTLAWS

I used to have a coworker named Lawman, he was an older gentlemen, he treated all of us in the office like we were his family. He was a wonderful man who had been screwed over in life; his wife had left him to raise his 3 children on his own. He did a great job; his whole life was about his children. Don't get me wrong, when his kids were older he would go to the strip joints with the younger salesman in the office and he could keep up, he was no saint. He was just a good hearted man. He died of lung cancer and I have never really forgiven myself for not going to the funeral and saying goodbye. Everyone in the office went but me; my fear was that I would lose control of myself and blubber like a baby, like I did at big Bill Hold's. After all I had sat beside the man for a year and a half before he passed.

I had a chance about a week before he died to go and see him but I declined, too afraid of how it would make me feel. A lot of silly phrases that Lawman used to say come back to me these days, "You don't pull down your pants to fart do you?" That was classic Lawman. The one thing he used to say that really made me chuckle was he referred to his In-laws as outlaws. I loved that one. I know there are some people who get along great with their in-laws and some people do not. I think I would fall somewhere in the middle.

I'm not sure how to explain my relationship with my in-laws. It is not bad or good. That's like asking somebody how your mood is. It's fine, I am not constantly happy and I am not forever depressed. I know that I could have made a little more effort over the years but I am not a sociable person. Once upon a time I would have considered myself a social butterfly but I also used to drink, I wonder if the two go hand in hand. My inadequate social skills may have been interpreted as a slight or snobbish behaviour and as a result the belief may be that I don't enjoy spending time with them.

My father in law is fairly quiet and for the most part out of the picture, he travels a lot with his job, recently spending up to six months in China. I feel that I should mention that he is Steve's step dad but that somehow does not seem relevant, he had been in his life since Steve was six years old, they had a turbulent period through his teen years but other than that they get along. Steve's biological father still lives in England so we don't see him. I have met him once and the kids never have. Oh, I better figure out a way to contact him and let him know about his son.

We have made a point of celebrating the little get togethers we have at the airport when my father in law flies through. My in-laws live a two day drive away now and it is not always easy to get out to see them. The kids have flown out a few times and we have driven a couple but as the kids get older yada, yada, yada, they are self-centered teenagers.

I guess you could say we didn't really get off on the right foot. Steve had dated one of the girls that worked at his mom's store and one night his mom had a get together for her employees. Knowing that his ex was going to be there put me off and I didn't want to go. She had a little bit of trouble with him no longer being her boyfriend you see. In the end we didn't attend the soiree. Jan (Steve's mom) later told me that it was not at all meant to make me uncomfortable, she was just having an evening with her employees to build the team spirit. I understood completely.

We went over to their house a great deal in the early days, playing pool, smoking and drinking until the wee hours of the morning. His aunt and her partner would often be there as they were avid pool players. There was a card game that we used to play called Queenie, it was an English thing don't ask, I can't remember how the game was actually played but there were three dishes that you had to put pennies into. So, first place got the dish with the most pennies then second and third got the remaining I think. We all had a good time playing. Looking back now we were all pretty close in those days.

I recall when we told everyone that we were getting married, my mother said that they would pay for the hall and she would make my dress, but she wanted to ask Steve's parents if they wanted to be involved as he was their only son, I think my parents were happy to have some help I'm sure it was an expensive undertaking at the time. Steve and I were happy to just have a gathering of close friends but my mother had insisted on a hall wedding. I wasn't complaining. We had a little meeting with both sets of parents and Jan and Andy were quick to offer to pay for the flowers and the cake.

I thought that was very gracious as traditionally it is the bride's family that foots the bill or the couple start their new life with a great deal of debt. But as it was their only child I guess they felt a need to be a part of it. Jan went so far as to take a floral arranging class and brought a board of boutonnieres to my wedding shower at my mom's house so that people could choose what they wanted.

The cake; it was unbelievable. I have never had and have resolved myself to the fact that I probably never will have a more delicious cake. Jan had known a woman who created wedding and birthday cakes in her spare time. It was very simple, two tier heart shaped, one tier was carrot cake and the other was chocolate. Not those cascading cakes you see in the windows of Portuguese bakeries but it was more suited to us.

By the time we got to the reception hall the 2 tiered heart shaped cake was leaning to one side as one of the tiers had sunk into the cake. It was comical. As I found out that day the more you sweat the small things the less you will enjoy the day. Overall our wedding was a wonderful day, a few times it went off track, my dad stepped on my train and when I yanked it out from under him he almost fell over, I laughed through my vows but ironically those are the memories that are the dearest to both of us.

Maybe we should have waited until we could pay for our own wedding and have all of the little touches I wanted my dream wedding to have, but when we found out that Jordan was on his way we decided to step it up. Don't get me wrong, I am grateful to my parents and in-laws for their help and it was a great time had by all. The roof could have fallen in on the reception hall and the only thing that would have mattered on that day was I was going to spend the rest of my life with Steve, and he with me.

I used to threaten Steve that I wanted to get remarried on our 20th wedding anniversary. He would always say, "No way." I secretly hoped that he would relent over time and I/we could do it all over again. The dress, the cake, the flowers and the photos, Steve's aunt and her partner took the pictures and we also got a set from everyone who took pictures that day. I know it wouldn't have been the same, I just wanted to try. And now… Well, it will never happen for me.

When the kids came along our lives changed. Jan wanted

to look after them or take them out for walks but Steve and I were so protective that rarely happened. I had not been close with my grandparents as they lived in Scotland my whole life, we would see them every other summer or occasionally at Christmas. So I didn't really understand the grandparent relationship. I think we all struggled with everybody's role.

At one point when Jordan and Katherine were toddlers, Steve and I decided to go back to school. The shitty grocery store or factory work was starting to get old and we wanted more for our new family. Jan and Andy, had just bought a big house but it looked like Andy was going to be relocated to Texas for his job. They weren't ready to let their house go, just in case they didn't like it in the south, and we needed a place to stay. We all thought this was perfect, Steve and I would sell our house, use the money for school, move into his parent's house while they were in Texas and they wouldn't have to worry about selling their house until they were settled in. Well, after selling our house the whole relocating thing fell through and we were all left to live in the house together.

It was difficult as anyone that has lived with another couple, family or person will tell you. Let's face it you can't run around the house naked, you have to make sure the bathroom doors are locked and you are conscious of every action. Well, maybe not everyone is like that but I am. Jan and Andy tried their best to make me feel comfortable but I still felt like I was a guest on a vacation that would never end. We had nowhere else to go so I didn't want to upset anyone.

To my horror one morning I found out just how hard it would be to keep that control. I got Katherine up for gymnastics; she was 3 at the time. This was my Saturday morning ritual. I would take Katherine to gymnastics where she could tumble and run around while I read a book in the quiet hall outside of the gym; parents weren't allowed in the gym, they were too much of a distraction for the little ones. I didn't realize how much of a distraction we were for my daughter until parent's day, she was so silly and didn't want to participate, she just rolled around on the mats.

On this particular day when we got back to the house after her lesson, it turned out that at some point Kathy had used black magic marker to draw all over her bed and the walls of her room. Somehow a permanent marker had made its way into the marker bin that Jordan and Katherine used for their crafts and that happened to be the marker that Kathy had used of course. She got in big trouble for that. It was awful I was living in somebody else's house and these were the kind of antics I was trying to avoid.

Sometimes it was something totally different like a communication breakdown. Before he found his love for hockey Steve and I let Jordan try out whatever sport interested him so that he could find one and stick with it. He would end up trying soccer, basketball, skiing, swimming and the list goes on and on. At four he had chosen soccer. Every Thursday at four o'clock he had his soccer lessons. I call them lessons because a bunch of four year olds running after a ball in a big swarm is not a soccer game, it is cute to see but it is not a game!

This one particular evening I told Jordan that he needed to get ready and I would be right back, I just needed something from upstairs. I was gone maybe five minutes and when I returned Jordan had disappeared. I called him and got no answer, I looked around the house calling his name and still there was no response. Then I realized his shoes were gone. Opening the front door I called him, no answer, I checked the car thinking that maybe he had went ahead and buckled himself in, he wasn't there. I looked up and down the street, no sign of him. I felt my stomach drop and frantically called for Steve. "Jordan's shoes are gone and I can't find him anywhere, I think he might have wandered off" I gasped.

Seeing that I was at the front door Steve immediately went to the back door, why didn't I think of that. He opened it seeing his mother down by the creek that the house backed onto, "Mum, have you seen Jordan?" He called to her. She couldn't hear him but bent down and Jordan popped his head up. Steve stormed out of the house and within seconds he was back with Jordan in tow, I was shaken but now able to take him to soccer.

Steve was yelling at someone. At first I thought it was Jordan he was hollering at but then I heard a woman's voice responding. It turned out that Jan had discovered a turtle down at the creek behind the house and took Jordan for a look not realizing that he had soccer. Steve was furious at the lack of consideration Jan had shown and she was just as furious at how he had treated her for something thought to be harmless.

After that life at the house was not fun. I tried to keep up appearances, we would all sit together in the basement and watch TV or eat the odd meal together, but most of the time I would go out or be in my room to avoid the tension. It didn't seem to be getting any better and it was becoming clear that we would need to find somewhere else to live, and fast, before we damaged our relationship beyond repair.

We moved out a few weeks later and ended up in a 2 bedroom basement apartment. The relationship remained strained for about six months but eventually as they say, time heals all wounds. My father in law had been offered a new job as President of a company in the West and we were asked to move back into the house, this time it was a done deal, they were re-locating and they needed someone to look after the house until it sold. We did move back in but only for 6 months, by then we were graduating college and getting back on our feet. We were able to get our own apartment and be independent once again.

It turned out the move out west was good for everyone and they still live there today. They will be in town for the funeral but will stay at Jan's sister's house. I really don't know what to expect for this afternoon. It will be very difficult for them both, it was their only son after all, I don't even want to imagine having to bury either one of my children, that would be the end of my world. I am glad that they are staying with her sister and not with us, I just need to be able to go to pieces whenever I want.

Note to self; I will have to look into taking a leave of absence from work. The thought of going back there anytime soon is unimaginable.

My company offers only 2 days bereavement. I am sure that they would be sympathetic as I have lost my spouse, but for how long. At some point I am going to be told to get my ass back to work. I am struggling with my existence right now, I can't fathom pissing precious life minutes away sitting in my cubicle while coworkers freak out over issues that I believe to be insignificant. Come on, I need to figure out what the point of this life is and how to leave my mark on this planet. Otherwise what is the point of our time here?

Steve never got to leave anything except a grieving family. I mean, I have heard that the best thing to do after losing a loved one is to go back to your normal life, so that means work for me, the kids are out of school for summer vacation and won't return for 2 months so they are already out of a normal routine. Oh man, and all I want to do is be with them.

I am afraid that I am in such a bad state that I will say the wrong thing to the wrong person. I need to be in control of my emotions today, especially my anger. Getting into a fight is not going to accomplish anything but a spectacle and that is not what I want this day to be about.

11 MORE OF ME

If this day isn't about me then why do I feel like I am making decisions based on my own selfish wants and needs. Why can't I just let Jan have her son sent off in a nice shirt and tie? Or call my sister back without being mad, these people have lost someone too. It is different for me though, they didn't see him every day when they opened their eyes, or countdown the last minutes of the work day until they could be in his presence again. I am tired of not getting what I want and giving into everyone around me.

I always back down even when I was in my teens, if I was getting in trouble I would shut my mouth until the lecture or screaming tantrum was over and just go to my room. Well I am done with that. Steve was my knight, he protected me from everything that hurt and now that he is gone I need to stand up for myself otherwise who will?

I pick up the phone and immediately dial Lisa. The phone rings twice then she answers, "Hello?" I take a deep breath and calmly say into the receiver, "It's me, listen this is a hard enough day can you please write down the God damn funeral info? I'll give it to you one more time, get a pen I will wait." The line goes quiet and I hear, "Uh, okay just a sec." When she returns I give her the time and hang up the phone. Maybe I should have been a little nicer I struggle.

Every thought every action seems to be in total contradiction to what I want to happen. "SHUT UP!" I yell out loud to my conscience. I wish I could kill that voice in my head, life would be a lot easier. I wouldn't be so soft. But what kind of a person would I be without it? Isn't that what separates the normal people from the mass murderers, a conscience. Right now I don't care, we can figure that out later. I return the phone to its cradle and lie on my bed staring at the ceiling. With that I revert to the old me and curl up into a ball literally and figuratively.

Well I think that is enough aggressive therapy for me, and if I am honest with myself that is not the person I want to be either. I just want to be treated with the respect I feel I deserve and not like a fuck up. I don't like me very much. I feel weak and lack confidence.

So what's wrong with me? I try to make everyone around me happy. The problem is that is impossible. From the smallest issue of what kind of bread to buy to bigger ones like who do I try not to hurt on this terrible day. Being this way is detrimental to my health because it doesn't matter how many people I am trying to appease am I ever content? The answer is no. When I think back on my life there are so many times that I missed out because I denied myself the right to be happy. If I had decided a long time ago to speak up then maybe things would be different now. Like the fear of confrontation, if I had dealt with that maybe I would be more confident and not so scared today. Scared of the confrontation as well as hurting other people's feelings. It is easier to manage my own disappointment than have to live with the guilt of someone else's.

I grew up in a middle class neighborhood. My parents both worked and instilled in me a good work ethic. I had everything that I needed and more. There was a pool in our backyard, family vacations to Disney and Myrtle Beach, and the occasional meal out. My cousins lived a fifteen minute walk away and we were all close enough in age to hang out. Oh God, my life was an eighties sitcom or drama depending on what year it was. I loved going to my aunt's house to see my cousins. We would sleep over and stay up all night.

My older cousin Ian is four years older than me and he introduced me to cool music. My younger cousin Thomas was like my brother as there are only five months separating us. While at their house we would indulge in Fruity Pebbles cereal and playing with Play Doh, it was awesome. I can even remember the smell of their house, it was a mixture of whatever cologne my uncle used and carpet fresh carpet cleaner.

The closeness we all had when we were young ended once we entered high school as cliques rule the world in high school. The three of them, my cousins and sister all seemed to hang out with the same people and were still tied together, while I ended up in a totally different group. In later years Ian would move to Florida and Thomas to Oklahoma, keeping in touch only occasionally.

I have never felt good enough when it comes to people. It's almost as if I went off the rails during high school and nobody ever gave me the guidance or tools to get back on track. Like everything I have ever done right doesn't count. That is bullshit, why do I feel this way? I have moments of great pride in myself. With two kids I managed to go back to College and graduate. Not just graduate, obtain the highest grades out of everyone in the program and obtain a medal as recognition. I am proud of that. I am sure nobody thought I would ever accomplish that. I am proud that I got to stay home with my children for the first five years of their lives and not have someone else raise my babies. I supported my husband no matter what he wanted to do and how scary it was for me because I believed he could be successful, and he was, because he wasn't chained to a desk and that is how he measured success.

That's the funny thing though, I am an intelligent person and I could have done anything with my life. It is sad because I know there are a lot of kids who experience what I did and there isn't a need for it. If you had to meet with your guidance counselor in school and they sat with you to identify the different subjects or hobbies that you enjoy then maybe more kids would be happy in their work. If I was given a little booklet that was divided into chapters by subject and it listed all of the professions in that subject, then I would have been aware of my different options and that could have changed my life. For example; one chapter is called Food and it lists every job from waitressing to a Michelin chef. But, I wouldn't want it if it meant that I didn't meet up with Steve nor have the kids. And really all of the hardship and struggle that we have been through has made us the people we are today. Well, made me the person I am today...

12 KILLING TIME

I stretch out horizontally on the bed and Mittens nuzzles into my side. I can feel her purring and I scratch under her chin. She loves to be scratched under the chin, and when you stop the line of her mouth turns up into what looks like a smile, it is very rewarding to be able to make a cat smile since usually they are such assholes.

I stare up at the ceiling enjoying the purring vibrations emanating from my companion. Exhaustion hits me hard and I close my sore swollen eyes. They sting as I shut them against the light. I turn on my side and put my arm over Mittens and she moves closer to me. She is so warm which I don't mind as the room is being kept cool from the humming air conditioning that is pumping frigid air through the vents.

I can feel myself slipping into unconsciousness. I am so tired, I didn't realize until this moment. I don't really want to sleep but my body suddenly feels as if it is made of lead and I can't move. I try to fight it, I try to focus on the million thoughts running through my mind of what is going to happen today, but in the end my fatigue wins and I surrender, albeit reluctantly to sleep. I start to dream….

I am walking through a desert surrounded by dunes that block the horizon, reminiscent of Salvador Dali's Melting clocks. I can't see anything but orange sand, the wind has picked up and I have to shield my eyes from the blowing debris. For some reason I turn to look behind me sensing someone's presence, there is nothing there. Even my footprints have disappeared in the blowing sand, I am overwhelmed by disappointment, my loneliness envelops me.

I curl into a ball and sit in the sand hugging my knees to my chest, I rock back and forth to soothe myself and keep my sadness at bay. It doesn't work. Sand starts to collect and cover me, I feel like I can't breath, the sand is getting in my mouth and I can't see anything but orange, within seconds it has cocooned me and the sand has become a hardened sarcophagus, I start to freak out, my claustrophobia taking hold, I pound my fists on the cocoon breaking it easily. I am able to poke through, the shell is now as brittle as an egg. I stand and look around me, the scene has changed and I am now in a beautiful meadow.

I step out of my now destroyed shell and walk through the grass. A path has been cut but the surrounding grass is thigh high, I run my hands through the long grass as I walk down the path that has been cut for me. I come upon a clearing and there is a man sitting at a picnic table with his back to me. He looks like my dead grandfather from the back. I call out to him and he gets up from the table and starts to walk away, never turning so I can see his face. I start to run down the path towards him and he moves faster away from me, I am confused by this action, "Why does he want to get away from me, where is he going?" I try to call out but I can't find my voice. I try to run faster but my feet won't cooperate. I fall in the grass, as I look up night has descended on the meadow. I am afraid of the sounds and what is lurking in the tall grass.

Again I have a feeling of a presence with me. I get to my feet and dust off my jeans. This proves to be a mistake as the sand I brush off turns into a mini dust devil right in front of me, so close that I can touch it. I am not afraid and I reach out my hand to touch it. A hand appears suddenly from the cloud and grabs my wrist. I gasp and try to pull away panic rising. The dust settles instantly and my grandfather has a death grip on my wrist, only he looks like a rotted corpse and not my beloved grandpa. I struggle to free my hand using the ground as leverage from his iron grip and get away but when I look again Steve has taken his place with his arms stretched out, he wants me to surrender to his embrace. I relent and he draws me into him. He is not a rotted corpse, Steve appears to be the beautiful handsome man that I married. I am so relieved to see him, he wraps his arms tightly around me.

Somehow we are now sitting on a large wing chair that we both fit in comfortably and I am on his lap with my head on his chest. I feel so safe and loved in this moment that I never want to leave. He reaches for my necklace, and I readjust to look into his face. It was his, and I remember him wearing it when I first met him, his father had given it to him before he left England as a child, except when he was young the charm was a St. Christopher medallion with "To Steve Love Dad" engraved on the back. I have worn it for the last twenty years with an ingot charm replacing the medal. He lets the ingot fall back to its place around my neck and pulls me to him. I again am resting my head on his chest, breathing him in. He kisses my head and then he is gone.

I am left in the dark on the dirt ground again, frantically looking for him and shouting inaudible words. My hands raking through the dirt as if he is an object I will find buried there.

I wake with a start, my pillow soaked with my tears and

my face is wet. I have been crying again, this time in my sleep and the end of my dream is still with me. He was there, I could feel him holding me. My heart is breaking all over again and the sadness weighs on me like an anvil. I lazily glance at my clock, it says it is 2:45pm. "Oh my God!" I jump up wide awake now, pulse pounding. How could I have slept so long? The car will be here in 15 minutes. I shake off the emotions of my dream; there will be time to analyze it later. Right now I have to haul ass.

I open my bedroom door with a shaky hand and call to the kids, "Guys you almost ready?" Katherine appears at her room door still in her pyjamas. I cock my head to one side and give her a look that says, "Really? You are not ready yet?" I fight to control the anger that has started to well up inside of me, taking a deep breath I say, "The car will be here in 15 minutes, will you be ready?" She nods but it is not very convincing as she disappears back into her room. I can hear Jordan's music cranked up and trying to escape from his bedroom. I walk down the hall and pound my fist on the door, knowing if I just knock at a normal volume he will never hear me.

The music cuts off mid scream and Jordan opens the door a foot. "Car will be here in 15 minutes will you be ready?" I ask noticing that his hair is wet, that is a good sign, it means he has been in the shower. "Yup, I'll be ready." He says reluctantly. I smile at him, I am thankful that even though this is something that none of us want to do at least we all realize it is something that has to be done.

I turn to Kathy's bedroom door, guilt seeping into my brain, and I knock softly, she calls for me to come in. "Sorry I was short with you Kathy, I just fell asleep and when I woke up all of my time was gone and we have to get ready and…" I trail off. She is smiling at me. "Okay, so 15 minutes." I say to her as she comes toward me and gives me a hug. I didn't know how much I needed that. I melt into the embrace and am reminded of Steve holding me in my dream. She really is a girl of few words. Our hug ends and I leave her room closing the door behind me.

My heart swells with a mixture of pride and love for my children. I can't imagine what my life would have been like if I had never had them. It blows my mind to think that there are people who make a conscious decision to not have children. I mean, to each his own, but that thought never crossed my mind. They truly are a mix of the two of us. Katherine takes after Steve's biological dad's side with her looks, the dark hair and blue eyes and her intuitive mind. Her maternal heart and compassion come from me. Jordan has an amazing memory and is charismatic. Both come from me but physically he is his father's double, just a bit taller and skinnier. They are both very intelligent that comes from Steve and me. They truly could do whatever their hearts desire. I hope they believe that and live a happy life.

I heave a big sigh and head back into my room. Time to pay the piper, a smile dances on my lips as I think of our wedding, we had a bagpiper, he had played Amazing Grace, it was so beautiful. After the service my sister was frantically looking for my mom as the piper needed to be paid. So in reality, I have already paid the piper. I give my head a shake, my brain is a nervous mess of memories and silly sayings, thank God there is only room for one in there otherwise I might end up locked up in a psych ward.

I take the dress still hanging on the door of my closet and move it to the towel rack in the en suite bathroom. Slapping some more moisturizer on my face, I will the swelling to subside and hope that I can look like myself again. My hair is a rats nest and I quickly tug out the knots with my hairbrush. "OW! It hurts." I would have jumped into the shower again, but I just don't have time. My hair has a slight frizz to it from being trapped in knots for the past 2 hours but only on one side, lovely!

I run my hand under the water and pat the untamed side down so that it behaves and is at least level with the nice side. I eye the mascara that is poking out of a canister on my side of the sink, I wonder to myself, "Should I risk it? It is supposed to be waterproof..." I ponder over this issue for another few seconds then decide, "Is now really the time to find out?" I abandon the makeup idea, I only wear it for special occasions but I am not usually crying at those events. I have just cut 5 minutes off of my getting ready time. Yay me!

I quickly shed my comfy clothes and pull the dress on over my head. Looking in the mirror I am impressed, I don't look as bad as I thought, my swollen patchy skin is settling down and the dress is actually complimentary to my shape. It is a little thing and may seem vain but if it helps me get through this day I will take it. Maybe I will get through this day after all. I think I have reigned in my emotions when a memory from my dream drifts back to me. I could feel him, smell him, he was there....

13 LEAVING

A horn sounds from outside. "Shit the car is here." I run down the stairs and opening the door see the black Lincoln parked on the street outside of our house. I give the guy a wave and yell, "Just give me a minute." He nods and settles in. Closing the door I wonder how many families this guy has seen take this drive?

"Car's here!" I yell up the stairs not really expecting a response. As I yell, Jordan rounds the corner at the top of the stairs and I end up yelling in his face. He backs away from my hollering and says, "Jesus Mom." For a moment my anger flares, like I knew he was coming around that corner at that precise moment. All the stars aligned and it was my chance to scream in his face, instead I say, "Sorry", and we move on.

He looks so handsome; he has on a button up white shirt with purple plaid lines and a lime green tie with black pants. I know it doesn't sound like it would work, but Jordan can pull it off. Unfortunately his face reflects the mood of the day. He looks older and the dark circles under his eyes can't hide the grief that he is suffering from. At that moment I realize maybe I was wrong, maybe Jordan is going to have a harder time without his dad than Kathy is. It is so hard to see Jordan this way as he is the joker, not taking life too seriously, it is deeply disturbing to have someone who is up all the time at this all time low.

As he gently pushes past me I wonder what will become of him. Because really now what is the point of working hard at school and getting an education if you can just drop dead on a trip to the liquor store. Why not just knock up your girlfriend and spend the rest of your life with the person that you are in love with at this moment in time? Well, because that may not be the person you are going to be in love with in 2 years, because it is not guaranteed that you will drop dead at 38 years old. Because even if you do drop dead at 38 don't you want to experience life and leave your family taken care of, and perhaps not be miserable for the last few years of your existence? These are all the things I want to say to him, and I will get a chance later, this is not the time or place.

Am I right? As parents we are always telling our offspring to wait. Finish school, wait until you're older, and go to college. Why? Shouldn't we all be living in the moment? How many hours of our lives do we spend waiting in lines, attending classes, closing cupboard doors or cleaning? Those last two were more for me than anyone else. I don't really want to know how much time I waste on these menial tasks because I think that would be depressing, but aren't I right? Shouldn't we be having more fun, getting outside and living life?

Everyone should allow themselves a day off occasionally, to be the one that spills the grape juice on the couch and not worry about it. There is one person in every family that carries the burden for all the members of that family, the scapegoat if you will. The person you blame if the house is a mess or dinner is burnt or your black pants aren't clean. I am that person. I think you become that person when there is no one else to fill that role.

Maybe that is why I check off the weeks on the calendar until my next vacation, because vacation is the only semblance of a break that people like us get. I don't think it is enough. We need more jump on the bed days, mental break days where someone else worries about feeding the dog or if something has been taken out for dinner. A normal day for me in the Andrews' house consists of:

Wake up - Walk the dog
Feed & water animals
Laundry
Work out
Get ready for work
Drive kids to school
Go to work
Make lunch
Take something out for dinner
Make dinner
Feed animals
More laundry
Run around city for whatever the kids are in need of
Walk dog - Go to bed

Katherine appears on the stairs and I am taken aback, I had been lost in my own thoughts. She has decided to wear her army green dress with a button up front and the pearl necklace that Steve's dad got her from one of his many trips to foreign lands. She looks beautiful with her dark hair framing her porcelain face and at the same time she looks comfortable. She descends the stairs and gives me a weak smile. "Oh Kathy, you look lovely." I say, and opening my arms pull her to me. She doesn't resist, she never does, Katherine is a cuddler. "Okay, shoes on let's get going." I say to them both just like I do every morning before we get in the car and head off to school.

Kathy sits on the Queen Anne bench at the front door

and pulls on her black Chuck Taylor's. A smile spreads across my face, of course she needs to put her own Katherine flare on her ensemble. I turn to Jordan who is standing next to me with his shoes already on and slip my arm around his middle giving him a squeeze. To my surprise he turns into me and gives me a big bear hug. I can feel his sadness weighing on me and I know that we are all going to need each other over the coming months.

How am I going to make this okay? Fighting the tears that again threaten I tap him on the back and he releases me. He hunches his shoulders and wipes his nose on the back of his hand. He won't look up but I am sure he is quietly crying. "Don't shake any hands with that one." I tease him, meaning the hand he has just smeared his mucus across, I see the corners of his mouth curl into a smile despite his sadness. That is what I do, when things get too heavy I joke. It may not seem appropriate but it works for me.

I open the door and again head out into the glorious day, all the while the sun is blazing overhead. It is so hard to comprehend what we have to face today when the day makes me want to skip, run or go for a swim, anything fun in the sun. The driver gets out and opens the back door for us. "Thank you" I say to him and climb into the car after Katherine and followed by Jordan.

The A/C is cranked, luckily as we are all in danger of becoming puddles; I am sweating from the short jaunt to the car. The driver closes the door and gets in the driver's seat. "And they're off" I think to myself and reach for a hand from each child and squeeze them gently in mine. Part of me is now relieved as this will be over soon, while the other part is worried about the coming event. I am nervous and when I feel this way I am goofy. It doesn't matter how many times you play a scenario over in your head, it never ends up being the same. I think right now though my relief is outweighing my worry, and I finally feel like myself for the first time today.

The church is the same one that we were married in and had the children Christened in. Since we don't formally belong to a congregation I felt it fitting to have the service there. Steve had always seemed to love the old church. We then have to drive the half hour to the cemetery and crematorium for the burning. I know I shouldn't say that but that is what it is. After that we will go back to the house and probably sit there for people to see, like animals in a zoo, I don't want to be gawked at. How do I get the stragglers to leave? Maybe I will just go up to my room. What would they do then? I think that is what I will do, it almost feels like a tribute to my late husband as something he would do, wander upstairs and lock the bedroom door. I will ask Jordan and Katherine to join me though; I don't want to desert them.

We drive through the city and I remember my sunglasses. I had made sure the other night to put a pair in my bag for each of us. I open the bag and hand Jordan and Katherine some shades. They put them on grateful for the physical barrier.

It doesn't seem like long before the car slows to a stop and I look out the window at the grey stoned building. St. Andrew's Presbyterian Church looms above us. I don't even know what Presbyterian is. Add it to my list for google.

I have always just thought of myself as non-Catholic. I think that was only because I didn't attend Catholic school. My mom told us that we were Protestant when we were young, if that were true why did we go to a building every week that declared us Presbyterian? Yes, not only did I attend church weekly until I was twelve years old I also was a member of the choir and participated in Christmas pageants, got to be a lamb one year. I did know how to read when she told us this but I never questioned it.

Where I came from you either went to the Public or

Catholic school. I can remember some of the ignorant Catholic kids yelling across the field something about the "public kids" they thought it was our religion. Wow, another generation of kids thriving on our education system.

Why are the schools always right next to each other? We would always have stand offs down at the tree line that separated the two schools. Rumours would run rampant about the possibility of a rumble, but of course it never came to fruition.

These stories used to terrify me and I was plagued by visions of bikers with thick chains clad in leathers and wearing bandanas on their heads. Snakes and lead pipes would also show up in my imagination. Sometimes the hype was so exaggerated that I would run all the way home not bothering to look back, too afraid of what I might see. Jeez, I must have been in great shape; that was at least a mile hike.

The driver parks on the street as you cannot pull up to the front door and the parking lot to the side of the building is only able to accommodate maybe fifteen cars. The church faces a quiet two lane road and sits about 100 yards back from the street. There are two walking pathways leading up to two sets of double wooden doors, I guess the architect was really into symmetry.

Our Chauffeur turns expectantly to look at us in the backseat. "I will be here at 4 O'clock to go to the crematorium" he announces. I manage a weak smile and thank him again. Katherine is sitting between me and the door with her hand on the arm rest. The driver then gets out and this time goes to Katherine's side of the car to let us out. He opens the door and I wait a moment and then say, "Okay Kathy let's go." She takes a deep breath and steps out of the car.

We are instantly surrounded by humidity, "God I hope

the church is air conditioned," I wish to myself. "Oh, don't say God" I scold myself. We all exit the car and start the long walk up to the double wooden doors that lead into the lobby which then opens onto the Nave. The closest pathway is the one to the right of the building. The asphalt walkway is bumpy from years of people trampling over it, losing its black sheen it is now more of a pitted grey.

I look at the lush green grass and remember standing on it at my wedding when Steve and I smiled for what seemed like a million pictures. At the end of the day our faces hurt and that just made us laugh more. I never thought I would be alone after that day, time has gone by so fast.

There are not many people walking up to the church; I assume they are already inside. I see my aunt as I am walking and she gives me a little wave as she enters the church. It is so awkward, are we allowed to wave and be happy to see each other? It just seems wrong to find any joy in this day and I feel guilty for smiling at her.

The Church bulletin that stands sentinel on the lawn declares an upcoming bake sale and Sunday's services are at 8 and 10. We approach the stone steps and I remember taking Jordan and Katherine's picture on these very steps at both of their Christenings, holding them in their little white gowns, now they are almost adults.

Walking through the doors there are people everywhere, none of whom I recognize, then I realize they are church volunteers ready to direct the human traffic that doesn't exist. For some reason they recognize me, I have no clue who they are, and they quickly offer me their condolences and send me toward the front of the church, apparently when your spouse dies you get front row seats, awesome!

I walk down the same aisle that I did when we were married. This time such a contrast dressed in black and flanked by my children, not my father. The coffin is in front of the altar and the cherry wood is gleaming under the lights. I don't really remember choosing that box from the list but it's a little late to argue about it now. Steve was partial to cherry I am sure he would be okay with it.

The three of us walk arm in arm to the front row, eyes forward, I don't want to meet anyone's gaze. Jordan and Katherine take their seats, I hesitate and go up to the coffin. I place my hand on the shiny wood exterior. The coffin is cool to the touch, I'm not sure what I was expecting, maybe to feel his presence somehow, but there is nothing. I pull my hand away unsatisfied. A fear gripping me and my imagination envisioning zombie Steve opening the casket and grabbing me by the wrist like my grandfather did in my dream.

I turn back toward the pew and for the first time I see the people who are staring at me. The church is maybe half full and I am stunned seeing faces full of pity and people whispering to each other. What are they saying, "Oh she looks fat in that dress", or maybe "She's aged a lot, time is a cruel thing", or maybe they are just waiting for me to lose it and break down.

I am full of anger and decide at that moment I will not give the ones who are here to see that the satisfaction. I will be strong and make Steve proud. By the same token maybe they are saying how strong I must be or how lucky to have the kids, it doesn't have to be all negative. I lower myself onto the cool wooden seat, once again between my children and removing my sunglasses I take a deep breath readying myself for the ceremony. The minister gives me a slight nod and heads for the pulpit, I think to myself, "Here we go."

14 TODAY

Two years have passed since the day of the funeral. A lot has changed; I will be 40 in a few weeks. I am lonely but I have the kids. I have thought of dating and came close, but have resolved myself to the fact that it is not an option right now. I still need time, it would feel like cheating still and I would never cheat on my husband. I have cemented a place with my parents, sister and nephew. It is nice to have somewhere to go when I get too sad and I don't want to drag the kids down. I have seen a kind of sadness on their faces that I would never want to see again.

It was a struggle for a good 6 months after he died. The insurance company didn't want to pay out his policy. I had to wait and then the paperwork was unbelievable, in the end they paid and I was able to buy a small townhouse and now live in a smaller City. I didn't want to disrupt our lives too much. So I bought Jordan a car and he finished his last 2 years of high school with his friends and will be attending college in the fall for culinary arts.

Katherine wanted to change schools and goes to the high school down the street from us, it is only a 15 minute walk as opposed to the hour she used to have to trek, so she can come home for lunch now. I sometimes worry that she is not being challenged in her new school; the old one had a good reputation for academics. She only has two more years of high school, then she will graduate and go on to University, she would like to be a pathologist. Fortunately Steve's life insurance policy will also help make that happen.

The house is paid for and I would really like to get a vacation place either up north in cottage country or down south on a beach somewhere, I could maybe rent them out and live off of the rent, that might just be a pipe dream but at least I have started dreaming again.

I am still working right now, although I have modified my hours and only work 5 hours a day. I bought a puppy and named him Scooby. Jordan has laid claim to him but in reality he is mine. He follows me around and knows who the boss is, in other words I feed him. I had to put Buster down last year, he was suffering from arthritis and in the end he could hardly walk. It broke my heart to see him hobbling around the house. I tried to deny it at first but in the end it seemed the only merciful thing to do. He had a good life and he was loved dearly, and still is.

I have become a lot healthier, even now I am thinking about making a salad to go with our supper. Katherine's vegetarianism has definitely rubbed off on me. We were good before but I have opened my mind to other things, except tofu, that stuff is disgusting! I go up to the local conservation centre on the weekend and hike through the woods. Last winter I finally took up cross country skiing with Katherine, she loves it and it was something I had been talking about doing for years. Talk is cheap, is a valuable lesson I have learned in the last two years. This year we plan on investing in some skis.

I am tired a lot more now, not sure if that is from the grief or getting older or it could even be because I am more active. I don't like to sit around like I used to because then my mind starts to work overtime and I am not a fan of the thoughts in my head. I start to question my existence and what is after death, I work myself into such a frenzy that I end up having a panic attack and struggle to breath. I used to have this problem before Steve died, but it has gotten worse.

My doctor tried to put me on medication but I find keeping busy is a lot more enjoyable, except for the exhaustion factor. I was never one to run to the medicine cabinet, I would rather tough it out, maybe that is why I seem to have such a high threshold for pain. Some people look at me as if I am crazy, we'll see who survives when the zombie apocalypse comes!

It's dinner time and I can hear Jordan and Katherine in the other room watching T.V. They have become a lot closer since their dad passed. I think they just found some common ground with their grief. It isn't unusual now for them to be talking to each other behind closed doors. I am so glad that they have each other.

Sounds like they are watching Wheel of Fortune, I can hear the ticking sound the wheel makes as it spins. I am just waiting for the pot of water on the stove to start boiling and then I can start the rice. Steve once said that I had perfected Uncle Ben's fine herb and wild rice. What can I say? It's a gift, open package, boil water.

Staring at the water I start to think of the absurdity of life. Somebody somewhere doesn't have access to drinking water yet I can flip on a tap and ta-dah! I think I read on the internet, my favourite pastime, something like 600 million homes in India don't have a toilet, however, the average person has a cell phone, what is that about? I don't get it.

I think I am the only person in the western world over the age of 12 that doesn't have a cell phone, and I am okay with that. When did life get so stressful, why do we have to be in contact every minute of the day? I enjoy being left alone occasionally to just do whatever I want and not have to compromise because of other people who happen to be in the room. Not always, just occasionally. Wow, I sound like a grumpy old lady. Next thing you know I will be yelling at kids to get off my lawn!

I had recently gone for my physical and pointed out to my doctor something weird in my left breast, she wasn't worried about it. For my own peace of mind I went for a test and lucky me I got to be fondled by a young technician wielding an ultrasound wand named Jenny. Jenny told me at the end of the test to "try not to worry about it" all due respect to Jenny, I think I will wait and see what my doctor has to say about it, ah the waiting game.

Not sure how many times in my life I have convinced myself I was dying or had a terminal disease. By no means am I a hypochondriac but when something is out of the ordinary then it can only mean a slow painful death. A mixture of fear and the internet are a very dangerous cocktail.

The doorbell rings and judging by how loud the TV is I know that I am the only one who can hear it. I sigh resolving myself to the fact that I still do everything around here. I poke my head into the hall; maybe I can identify who it is at the door by their silhouette, but not today. The frosted glass just lets me see the outline of a man a bit taller than me wearing a baseball hat. "Jesus" I mutter under my breath annoyed to be disturbed right in the middle of making dinner, convinced that it is going to be someone peddling their wares, I don't want to subscribe to a newspaper, I can get the headlines on the web for free.

I grab the dish towel slung over the stove handle and wipe my hands. Throwing it over my shoulder I head to the door, shooing Scooby out of the way, he has decided to lounge horizontally in the hallway over one of the heating vents, it's not even that cold, "Baby" I hiss at him. Just as I put my hand on the door knob my visitor is now knocking on the glass and I grumble, "Hold your freaking horses" ever the passive aggressive, I swing the door wide to scare my unwanted visitor and standing there is what looks like an emaciated homeless man.

I have achieved my goal as he was shocked by my abrupt door opening, a look of surprise shows on his face. Then he breaks into a closed mouth smile starting at his lips crinkling his slightly tanned weather beaten cheeks until it reaches his eyes.

Those eyes, there is something vaguely familiar about them. His dirty clothes are hanging off of him and they are not appropriate for the season, they are warmer as if made for winter in the far North. He is wearing layers upon layers; it's almost as if he has on his whole wardrobe.

He is staring at me expectantly with that smile on his face and those piercing blue eyes, I feel like he is trying to will a message into my brain telepathically. "Yes?" I ask expectantly. He looks like I have cut him to the quick with the words that have just come out of my mouth. His face falls, the smile no longer on his lips he looks dirty and mean.

I can feel fear prickle the back of my neck and I am asking myself, "Why did I open the door?" I don't always open it although I have been forcing myself to lately, one of those face your fear things.

The man doesn't say anything just adjusts one of his many collars and the look on his face turns to one of deep sadness. He sighs, and heaving his load he turns to go. He looks over his shoulder at me as he steps down the first stair. Something about that look hits me. Those blue eyes such a contrast with the rest of his shabby appearance.

He is wearing a beat up ball cap that says Leviathan, you can tell it was once black but it is now a kind of grey with a faded green beak. "Steve had a hat like that." I think to myself. "Wait" I say to the figure descending my front porch, uncertainty has taken over. He turns and the smile has returned to his face. This time I can see his teeth a little bit. A memory of Steve decked out in his hunting gear comes to mind.

I examine the man a little closer and I cautiously take in his appearance. He is about 6ft. Maybe he looks older than 40 but that may be the grime. He is broad and muscular looking but it is hard to tell with all the layers. His hands look rough and callused as he rests one on the railing. I look up in disbelief and realize who I am looking at but it can't be. "Steve?" I gasp.

He has started back towards me, his blue eyes now filling with water, the smile is back and he is nodding. The foyer has started to spin, I need to sit down but I am trying to comprehend what is happening grasping the door handle for support. "It's me Hon" is his reply. That is his voice, but this person doesn't look like my husband. Wait a minute yes he does, THE EYES! This can't be real we set him on fire, how can he be here? He died, we mourned him. What the hell is going on?

I can feel the panic rising in the back of my throat making it feel like it is threatening to close off my wind pipe, my heart is racing, beating too fast. How many times have I woken up with this feeling? My head is reeling. I am not sleeping this time though I am wide awake. I feel lightheaded as if I am leaving my body. Darkness has crept into the edges of my vision, oh God I am hyperventilating. A painful thunderclap rips through my temple on the left side. My head is swirling faster now; I'm going to pass out. I fight against the feeling; I don't want him to go, afraid that if I pass out he will be gone again when I come around.

I can hear the smoke detector going off but it's as if I have a pillow over my head and it sounds far away and muffled. "The rice" I remember and turn towards the sound but that was a mistake, pain rips through my head, feeling as though I have been struck by a sledgehammer. The hallway is in full tilt now and I can't do anything but try to swim against the unconsciousness that is closing in. I bend at the waist putting my hands on my upper thighs and shuffle my feet apart trying to keep my centre of balance and stay upright. It is no use, within seconds I am falling.

I can see the doorway rushing past my eyes in a blur, Steve's figure is still there reaching for me. "MOM!" I hear Jordan screaming followed by, "Get the fuck outta here what did you do to her?" He is running down the hallway towards me, I hear his footsteps and assume the smoke detector has roused him out of his television trance. Scooby is frantically barking unsure what to do but sensing Jordan's unease; he is too chicken to attack the stranger who is now in our foyer.

I hit the tiled floor hard and see 3 blurry shapes over me, a buzzing has filled my ears and I can feel warm liquid pooling around my head. "It's your dad" I manage to stammer, then the darkness takes me.

15 THE HOSPITAL

Standing under the harsh glare of the fluorescent hospital lights the smell of disinfectant invading my nostrils I keep replaying the commotion that had unraveled just half an hour earlier.

I had expected a warm homecoming but she hadn't recognized me. Then when she did the look of confusion that was on her face hurt. Did she want me to be dead? Why couldn't her reaction have been elation that I had returned? I guess I did have some explaining to do. When the doctor comes out I will ask to see her and tell her I did it for the money, the insurance money so that we could get our lives back on track. I couldn't stand to look at her depression ladened face anymore. She was so unhappy and pissed off with life before I left.

I never imagined our reunion going this way. At least a thousand times I had played out this scenario. She would open the door and recognize me right away, well that didn't happened did it? Then she would be so happy to see me that she would melt into my arms, we would kiss and I would vow never to leave her again. And I wouldn't, the last two years on my own have been hell. On more than one occasion I just wanted to say fuck it and come home, just turn myself in.

Katherine had called 911 while Jordan tried to rouse Payton from unconsciousness. I checked for a pulse and held her tiny pale hand in mine. When the ambulance arrived Jordan jumped into the vehicle with his mother refusing to leave her side. A period of shouting ensued as I wanted to go with her. I hadn't seen her, touched her or been near her in two years. All I wanted to do right now was be with her.

Jordan was bordering on hysterical, the attendants took control telling me which hospital and to follow in my car with his sister. In the commotion I had forgotten about Katherine and turned to see her in the doorway looking very vulnerable and terrified. We followed in their mom's little navy blue Ford Focus at times tailgating the ambulance. Conversation was strained as we were both just concentrating on finding out what had happened and getting to the hospital, but Katherine new quickly what I had done and was dealing with her emotions internally.

Again I played the scene back, Payton's pupils had dilated and she seemed to lose her balance, grabbing onto her knees for support, I thought she was just hyperventilating until she finally keeled over. When she landed I thought her head had caught the corner of one of the tiles and that is where the blood came from but when the paramedics put her on the gurney I didn't see any cut, it wasn't making any sense.

As we turned into the hospital we passed the ambulance that had pulled up to the special door that only they can use and headed off in search of a parking spot. We quickly parked and half ran half walked up to the double automatic doors.

The waiting room was relatively quiet. Katherine sat and perched herself in a chair looking small and grey and saying nothing, her body language was as silent as her voice. I guess after all this time I seemed like a stranger or I have done something unrepairable, not something I can deal with tonight.

I approached the front desk and blurted out, "They just brought in my wife." The nurse behind the counter eyed me over her glasses and asked, "Name?" For a brief moment I wasn't sure if she meant mine or Payton's so I settled on our surname, "Andrews". She typed something into her PC which seemed to take forever and then told me, "She is in triage, just have a seat then someone will come for you shortly."

I couldn't sit down, the anxiety was too much and I would have been shaking my legs so bad that I'm sure I might have worn a hole in the floor.

The smell of disinfectant still invading my nostrils and now upsetting my stomach, I don't know how much longer I can keep it together. I had at least thrown off my jacket and sweater in the panic at the house and I was grateful for it now pacing the floor. The extra weight would be exhausting and would cause me to overheat.

The thought of my clothes makes me suddenly feel self-conscious and I can see people shrink away from me as I pace close to them. I must look like a homeless man. The crew neck collar of my shirt is worn and frayed, my jeans are ripped and stained from various objects, mostly dirt and grass but there is some blood on there too from the last time I hunted. My hair is long and straggly and my unshaven face does not resemble the well kept beards of the middle class dotting the waiting room.

A couple of years in the wilderness and you don't care about your appearance. There is nobody to impress. I had fantasized over the years about cleaning up before coming home but when I found where they were I could think of nothing but making the trip home.

The doors swing open mechanically and I turn to see my

Son stumbling through them, he beelines for his sister and collapses in the chair next to her. She visibly relaxes at the sight of him. I walk over to stand in front of them. Jordan has his head in his hands Katherine has turned towards him and put a comforting hand on his now hunched back. "Jordan" I say to him softly and that is his undoing, his body is now shuddering under Katherine's little hand. He crumples further forward so that he is bent completely in half and his arms are across his legs. I touch his head and comb my fingers through his hair in a comforting gesture.

He has grown so much I realize for the first time. Taller than me and he has the beginnings of a blond moustache on his upper lip. The doors swing open again and an older man with a white coat and equally white hair approaches us. He has a clipboard in his hand and he eyes me questioningly. Jordan rises up when he hears the door. His face is streaked with tears, he looks more like a young man than a teenager.

"Are you a relative?" the doctor questions me, "It says here the spouse is deceased." I just nod. "Let's go into this room over here." He herds us towards a door with a glass frosted window in it. It has a small sign in gold letters that says Family Room. Katherine reaches out to me and I fold an arm around her shoulders. "Can we see her?" I ask with hope in my voice which is quickly dashed once he turns to look at me. I know that something is not right. How could this day have turned out so wrong? I had been dreaming and fantasizing about this day, looking forward to it with every ounce of my being for the last two years.

We enter the dimly lit room and see that it is nothing more than a room with a few chairs and a wooden table. It seems very depressing. The doctor closes the door for us then turns again to face us. "I'm sorry" he starts. "Your mother has had a cerebral hemorrhage. Her brain had a clot that ruptured and has suffered severe damage."

Katherine starts to sob loudly, Jordan slumps into a

nearby chair and I cannot feel my legs. It's as though someone has taken the floor out from under me. "Wh-what does that mean?" I ask, "Is she going to recover?" The doctor shakes his head. "I'm sorry we just don't know the extent of the damage, she is on life support right now, we need to do some tests and possibly remove her from the life support to see if she responds. An MRI will show where the bleeding is coming from and we will then have to do surgery to stop the bleeding. Once we have the test results we will know more. A nurse will be in shortly to have you sign a consent form to remove her from life support temporarily."

I push my fingers into my eyes and see the flashes behind my lids. Jordan steps toward me and hugs me, it feels as if he is a drowning man and I am his life preserver. I motion Kathy to join us and in that moment we are one.

After a few minutes the nurse comes in with the paperwork and I sign it. They all seem to think that I am Payton's brother.

A couple of hours has passed and the doctor has come back with news. "We can see from the MRI that there is extensive bleeding on the brain. We will need to get her in the OR and see if we can stop it." I just nod, words escape me.

We continue to wait in the family room. We huddle together in a corner, nobody is talking, we are all just waiting, it's taking all I have to not vomit.

The doctor finally returns with a scowl on his face. "The bleeding was in difficult and multiple areas, we could not stop it." These words seem to echo through me. 'My God, no!' I think to myself. "What now?" Jordan asks before I can. After a long pause the doctor responds with great compassion in his voice, "Well, she is technically brain dead, she will not recover. Do you know if she is an organ donor?" I feel as though I have been punched in the gut.

Everything is spiralling out of control, what is happening. For the first time Katherine speaks up, "Yes, it's on her license." I am numb, I have lost her. There will be no waiting a year or two to find her healthy. She is gone. "No." Jordan gasps, "You can't do this, we will keep her on the respirator." Jordan looks pleadingly at me. "I'll give you a few minutes" the doctor says and exits the small room. I guess it is up to me to persuade my Son that his mother is already gone. I don't want her to be dead either. She can't live if she can't even breathe on her own. "Jordan" I say softly. He looks at me tears running down his cheeks. "We have to let her go. She can't come back." Again he buries his face in his lap. I pull him to me and we hold each other up.

Because she had her organ donor card we would get another hour with her to say goodbye as they need to keep the organs working as long as they can before they are removed and the surgeon is not ready yet.

We enter the hospital room to the beeping and chugging of machines keeping her body working. The left side of her face has become swollen and purple and her eye looks as though it is protruding from the socket, even though her lids are closed a line of white can be seen through her left one. I immediately wish that I had not come into this room to see her like this. I would have gladly held onto the visions in my head, her sunny blond hair and carefree smile, the way she would look at me as if there was no one else in her world.

Tears spring to my eyes and I tense my jaw trying to hold them back. The kids are sobbing, Jordan has clutched her hand holding it to his face. I notice she is wearing her wedding band and engagement ring. How many times had I teased her about not wearing them when she had taken them off to wash her hands and forgotten them by the sink? Here I had been "dead" for two years and she was holding on. Katherine had a death grip on my hand she seemed repulsed by the person in the bed. I think she felt her mother was already gone.

We stayed with Payton for a while and then a nurse came in and said, "I'm sorry but it is time." I move to Jordan and pull him gently away from his mother, he doesn't resist. I place an arm around each child and walk them down the hall and out of the ER double doors to the car. It was time to go home.

A few days have passed and I find myself waking up in her bed, the sunlight streaming through the blinds. I can smell the Sweet-pea body lotion that she always wore. Although this is not a room we ever shared, she is everywhere, and it feels familiar.

Scooby the German Shepherd is lying on her side of the bed. He turns and licks my face. We have gotten to know each other a little over the past few days. This brings a smile to my face but it is short lived.

I swing my legs out of the bed and sit up rubbing my face. It looks like a beautiful day outside, but for me and the kids this is going to be the hardest one of our lives. I never thought I'd live to see the day of Payton's funeral.

THE
END

ABOUT THE AUTHOR

Nicole Paton Schofield is an award winning amateur photographer, busy mom of two and a marketing associate at a large public company. She is currently enrolled in the University of Toronto's writer's craft course and is a graduate of the world renowned Sheridan College. She resides in the city of Mississauga just outside of Toronto, Ontario Canada with her two teenage children, her husband of almost twenty years, their two dogs, Sam and Buddy, along with their grey tabby cat Cocoa.